Rabbitman

Friction Fiction

Rabbitman by Michael Paraskos

First published by Friction Fiction 2017
an imprint of the Orage Press
16a Heaton Road
Mitcham
Surrey CR4 2BU
England

Special thanks to Lara Benjamin and the real Angela Witney.

ISBN: 978-0-9957130-0-0

Rabbitman

Michael Paraskos

For Ben

x

"Disrespect invites disrespect."

– Meryl Streep

§1

But I digress. What I meant to say was, once upon a time it always snowed at Christmas. In England I mean. I know in some places it still snows at Christmas. All year round even. But I digress.

The point is, once upon a time it always snowed in England at Christmas, like in a fairy tale. And it was snowing when our story is set. So, I suppose, that means this story is set once upon a time. And that it might be Christmas. Which might imply it is a fairy tale. Or a fantasy. Did I say fantasy? Yes, that's a good word. I suppose this book is a fantasy, an escape from the real world into a world of make-believe. And who doesn't need an escape like that every once in a while. A bit of escapism while you lie naked in your bed, reading. But on that thought, I digress.

Once upon a time it was 1978, and it was around Christmas time. It was snowing, but the snow didn't bother Angela. Are eight-year-olds ever bothered by snow? Maybe sometimes. But for Angela, eight years old, the sight of the white sheet stretching across the landscape filled her with happiness. She had been out early that morning, throwing snowballs at parked cars and trees and other inanimate objects in the absence of anything, or anyone, else to throw them at. And she had built a rather lopsided snowman. Angela's mother had refused to waste a carrot for the nose of her daughter's icy golem, but Angela had been allowed to take two pieces of coal from the coal shed for its eyes, and she had improvised its other features with broken sticks. Afterwards she had traipsed though a field where the snow was so deep it reached the top of her boots and soaked her feet inside. And she had enjoyed every second of all this, at least until her feet were wet. Then she felt suddenly cold and uncomfortable. So she had gone inside, where her mother gave her a pair of dry socks, put her tiny Wellington boots by the fire to dry, and sent her upstairs to play.

So, when our fantasy, our once upon a time, really starts, Angela was sitting inside, upstairs as instructed, on the landing of the tall nineteenth- century gothic-revival school house, in a tiny North

Downs village in southern England. There she was surrounded by what would have looked, to any casual passer-by, like a mountain of soft toys. Or do I mean a lake of soft toys? I'm not sure what I mean. Perhaps there is a collective noun for soft toys, but if there is, I don't know what it is. A plush of soft toys? But I digress.

The point is, the plush of soft toys was not piled up beside Angela, like some cotton and kapok mountain; it was spread out around her. To be more precise, the toys were seated around her, like an expectant audience looking at the main turn in an arena. No, I don't mean an audience. I mean they were like a theatrical cast in a rehearsal room, seated around the director of their play, awaiting instruction.

The landing, where the cast of this play was sat, was a strange place. It was, as you would expect, at the top of the stairs, and there it formed something like a meandering corridor. I am not sure how else to describe it anyway. To the right of the stairs it led to Angela's parents' bedroom and to the left, to the bathroom and toilet. A spur from

the left led to Angela's sister's room, and on, up
another flight of stairs, to the attic room shared by
Angela's three brothers.

Nothing so odd about any of that you
might think, except to wonder where Angela
herself slept. Well, Angela was a timid child, and
from infancy, until now aged eight, she had always
slept in her parents' room. She was, in truth,
terrified of the dark, and her parents were, in
effect, her comfort blanket.

But there was something odd about the
landing itself. Just before the door to Angela's
parents' room, another spur broke away and
formed a kind of balcony, running above the stairs,
but leading nowhere in itself. Or leading nowhere
obvious to sight. Indeed, if you looked along that
balcony you might have said it ended at a wall, in
which was set an arched window, out of which you
could see the front garden, covered in snow, a
gnarled old apple tree in the front yard, and the
main street that ran through the village. But
nothing more. Perhaps it is too fanciful to suggest
this strange extension of the landing was a liminal

space, as you would expect a liminal space to reveal two worlds, the one you are in, and the one you might enter. But after a while, perhaps you might think, actually this is a kind of liminal space, a very special liminal space, this functionless corridor, sitting between a world we inhabit and a world so unlike our own, we cannot even see it. Otherwise why have a corridor that led to nowhere? It must have led to somewhere. And I suppose it did. It led to Angela.

Young Angela used this landing balcony as her playroom. It was her only private place in the entire house. The only room of her own, a private space in full view of everyone who passed up or down the stairs. There she kept her menagerie of stuffed animal toys, from teddy bears and rabbits, to penguins, and an indeterminate number of mice-like creatures. There was an emu and a clanger, and an array of cats and dogs, and a camel, and an elephant, and a large toy turtle, and – well, and many more. Not all of them were stuffed toys, of course. There was a rubber toad, called Toady, and Mr Floppy, a stringed wooden puppet. There was Nou Nou too, and hundreds of plastic toy soldiers inherited from her much older brothers. And there were two dolls, one like a human baby that gave Angela the creeps, and the other a fake Sindy doll, bought for Angela by a distant aunt a couple of Christmases ago, from a stall at Herne Bay market. And there was much else besides. In short, Angela was spoiled for choice when it came to toys, and so, having far too many to play with individually, she had developed group activities in which they could all join in. It kept everyone occupied.

Angela's favourite group activity was performances, not so much plays, to be watched by other people, but participations, like Stuart masques, or mediaeval mystery plays, in which the participants were the audience, and the audience the participants. In this way, Angela's toys became actors in epic sagas, mystery plays revealing the eight-year-old's desires and fears, albeit only ever to herself and the plush of soft toys around her. It was this that took Angela beyond that corridor on the landing that led to nowhere, into invisible other worlds and imagined lives.

So now, those same toys were seated around Angela, awaiting direction to play out the latest fantasy that possessed her mind in that unnerving old house.

'Rabbitman,' said Angela, holding a soft toy rabbit, looking more like an upright hare than any bunny. 'I have a role for you. You are going to play President Rabbitman.'

'At last,' said Rabbitman, looking at Angela over the rim of his spectacles, whilst holding the script in his paws. 'A suitable part for my talents.' The other toys looked at each other, raising their eyebrows. 'And what sort of president am I?' continued Rabbitman. 'I mean, what is my motivation? I really need to understand my motivation.'

'Your motivation is power,' replied Angela. 'Doing a deal and profiting from it. There's no altruism in you. You are in it for yourself. Only for yourself.'

'Like he said,' mumbled Bobbi, 'a suitable role.' The other toys giggled, but Angela and Rabbitman ignored the jibe.

Turning to the other soft toys around her, Angela said, 'Rabbitman has been in power a long time, and has changed the country out of all recognition.'

'And what country is this, might one ask?' interrupted one of the toy rabbits, called Bunny.

'The country is Freedonia,' said Angela. 'And Bunny, I am going to place you are at the heart of Rabbitman's powerful inner circle.'

* * *

The old Freedonia was dead. Long dead. There was no doubt about that. The nation had registered the fact itself eight years earlier when it elected Rabbitman to the highest office in the land. And it had danced on the grave of the old Freedonia when it elected him for a second time four years later. That was why there were relatively few complaints, except from the usual suspects, when Rabbitman proposed a new law to abolish the country around him, and found a new nation in his own image. Thus Rabbitman was the last President of the Union of Freedonia, and the first President of the Federacy of Freedonia. So there was no doubt the old Freedonia was dead. Easy D as Rabbitman once said to the bemusement of his audience.

* * *

'Yes, I am getting the motivation now,' interrupted Rabbitman. 'My character sees himself as powerful, but he's also smart. He's smart and he knows he's smart.'

'But no one else thinks he's smart,' said Angela.

'Like I said,' mumbled Bobbi again.

'That's right,' agreed Rabbitman. 'No one else thinks he's smart. But they are just losers.' Rabbitman looked pointedly at Bobbi, put his paw to his forehead and used the stubby digits there to form the letter L, for loser, as best he could with paws instead of hands and fingers. 'Too bad!' he added laughing. 'I think, to mark this Triumph of the New Federacy my character would have overseen some remodelling at the presidential palace.' As Rabbitman said this, like an army of ants, the plastic toy soldiers pulled forward a large cardboard box, in which Angela had cut out windows and a door, to form an improvised dolls' house.

'Yes, the old palace in Freetown had to be remodelled,' continued Rabbitman. 'Of course, it would have been done in the best possible taste. I would have instructed my designers to use the glitzy Hare Building as their guiding model. The white stucco, and pokey rooms, and classical facade of the old Dolls' House would be swept away by President Rabbitman, and in its place a new golden dolls' house erected. Glistening every night in a panoply of artificial lights, it would be a huge erection!' The other toys sniggered, but Rabbitman ignored them. 'Let's be honest,' he said. 'It's a brutal symbol of the new Freedonia I have created.'

'You are right,' agreed Angela. 'That's exactly what President Rabbitman did. He pulled down the historic old Dolls' House and replaced it with a new golden Dolls' House. He even called it the Gold House, and when the usual suspects complained – the capital's elite who stopped listening to the people a long time ago – and threatened to take Rabbitman to court for destroying the nation's heritage, he just said it wasn't him. "Fake news!" he shouted, and everyone believed him.'

'Like I say,' said Rabbitman. 'He's smart.'

* * *

You see, President Rabbitman had to demolish the old Dolls' House. It might have been two-hundred years old but, as he told parliament, 'What was good enough for all those previous leaders of Freedonia is not good enough for me. I am now the most important rabbit in the world. So my house should look like it belongs to the most important rabbit in the world. Okay?'

What Rabbitman didn't mention to parliament was that it wasn't really his idea to demolish the old Dolls' House. It was the idea of his sixth wife, Bunny, who also happened to be his daughter. Bunny wasn't going to live in some grotty old stately home. Bunny wanted everything shiny and bran-spanking-new. And Bunny got everything shiny and bran-spanking-new. The only exception to this rule being Rabbitman himself. He was her father and her husband, so was clearly very, very old. So old, he had been alive before she was even born, a fact that so astonished Bunny she sometimes doubted it. But at least Rabbitman had money: lots of money. And it's easy to make lots of money look shiny and bran-spanking-new. So as long as her daddy-husband had money, and was willing and able to make everything else in her life shiny and bran-spanking-new, Bunny was willing to put up with his ancientness.

* * *

'What are you doing up there?' asked Angela's mother calling from the bottom of the stairs. 'Who are you talking to?'

'Rabbitman,' Angela called back. 'He's about to be sucked off by his daughter.'

Angela's mother returned to the kitchen, wondering if she had heard right.

* * *

Bunny licked Rabbitman's ancient penis a few more times, almost wringing it like a wet rag with her paws afterwards to make sure she had taken all his semen into her mouth. She then looked up at him with her big rabbit eyes, topped by long black lashes, and give the obligatory smile he always demanded. She opened her mouth a little to prove it really was full of Rabbitman's watery excretion, closed it again and made a theatrical show of gulping. This performance ended with her crawling up Rabbitman's ancient body to kiss him on the lips. Bunny's blow jobs on her father always ended this way, and had done so since long before they were married. Even when Bunny was a very little bunny, Rabbitman had insisted on it. He liked to taste his own semen in her mouth, and would wash his tongue greedily around her lips and teeth and gums, as though his own penile discharge was the real source of his power.

Having finished this ritual, Rabbitman washed, dressed, and left Bunny alone in her room in the Gold House. They no longer shared a bedroom. Bunny had said it was because of the late hours Rabbitman kept, ruining her beauty sleep, but the truth was more simple. Bunny wanted a private space to entertain the entertaining young bucks who formed Rabbitman's security guard. Tonight, once Rabbitman had gone, she had a special entertainment planned, with six of the best bucks from the Sixty-Sixth Detachment, none of whom would she have to wring out like a wet rag. It was her special treat to herself for Christmas Eve.

Moving downstairs, Rabbitman settled himself on his favourite comfy chair in the Rabbitman Room, the name he had insisted, on first becoming leader of the New Federacy, be applied to the main office of state. He looked into the flames of the roaring log fire in front of him, which seemed to burn with a particular intensity that night, making the silk-lined walls, shot through with almost as much gold cord as worm-woven thread, glisten in the flickering light. Leaning back in his chair. Rabbitman looked up to the ceiling, past the newly installed gilded plaster angels in the cornice, each looking more like a chubby cupid than any creature of heaven, and onto the ceiling proper. The equivalent room in the old Dolls' House had been decorated with no more than a plaster rose, surmounted with a Golden Eagle, symbol of the defunct Union of Freedonia, and was all painted white. In the Rabbitman Room the equivalent ceiling was painted with a neo-Baroque spectacular, showing the Ascendency of Rabbitman. In the *trompe-l'oeil* image more chubby cherubs could be seen supporting clouds, on which stood a somewhat svelte version of Rabbitman, ascending to the heavens in the company of a flock of brassy Federacy Eagles, each carrying the flag of the Federacy in its beak, and looking like it had just flown in from the back of an Alabama Klan pick-up truck. Sitting in front of the roaring fire, Rabbitman looked up and smiled at his own presence in the fantastical world he had created.

Apart from the burning fire, there was little other lighting that night in the Rabbitman Room. A desk lamp, with a green glass shade, was lit on the president's desk, but the only other source of light came from a pair of golden candelabras. These had been given to Rabbitman by the King of Englandshire, George VII, shortly before the king had fled into exile, and re-designated himself the King of Australia. The candelabras had been made for Louis XVI of France before his untimely firing at the hands of the French people, and each comprised a burnished bronze putti, this time making no attempt to mimic anything angelic, above which rose a golden foliate spray, topped by a golden herm in the style of an Egyptian sphinx. On top of each herm sat a golden splayed wax tray and a fluted golden candle holder, and on either side of these, two swirling golden foliate arms branched out, one left and one right, each ending in another golden sphinx's head, again supporting golden candle holders on their golden heads.

Of course Rabbitman had never really liked the King of Englandshire, although he had tolerated him becoming King of Australia. The king had upset Rabbitman by airing his views in public on Rabbitman's agreement with Emperor Vlad the Impaler, to carve up the oil rights in Antartica. Rabbitman was easily riled by criticism, and had used particularly colourful language to question the right of a third-world monarch to lecture him, the most important rabbit in the world, on the rights of a few surviving penguins. That was probably why Rabbitman had stopped supporting the king's desire to keep his kingdom intact, and instead covertly backed the break up of Britainnia into a Scotch Republic, a Welsh Rarebit and an Irish coffee, as well as Englandshire's unceremonious departure from the European League, a process dubbed *Fuxit* by the press. This left behind only a much-diminished English Mustard, renamed Englandshire, in the hands of its newly-installed brown-nosing leader, Balloonhead – at least until he also fell from power as Englandshire became ungovernable.

Yet, those original 1785 Louis XVI golden French candlesticks were some of the most highly-prized gifts Rabbitman had received during his presidency. That was why he had wasted no time having holes drilled in their antique bases, new electric lamp heads installed, and the revamped lamps placed in the Rabbitman Room.

Rabbitman looked at all this and for the most part he was happy. He had done it. He had made it. He had gone from being the ordinary son of a powerful multi-millionaire, into the most powerful man in the world, and a multi-billionaire. He was the ultimate man of the people, the self-made man, the man you aspired to be, at least if you were smart. Smart like him. Rabbitman often told people he was smart. It was the smartest thing he had ever done, as stupid people often believed him. And now everyone in the world knew he was smart. Only losers still denied it. As Rabbitman thought this he instinctively placed his fingers on his forehead to form the letter L for loser. It was an old trick from his first campaign trail. Playing to the pit. He chuckled at the memory of it.

* * *

'I almost forgot,' said Angela, standing suddenly. 'I need Balloonhead.'

'Who's Balloonhead?' asked Bobbi.

'You'll see,' replied Angela as she ran down the stairs. A few moments later she returned with a bright yellow balloon, floating senselessly on the end of a string. It wasn't a fancy balloon, in the shape of Mickey Mouse, or Scooby Doo, or anything like that. It was a very ordinary yellow balloon, almost too dull to notice except someone had hand drawn onto it a smiling face with a thick brown marker pen. There was something grotesque about that face, the two eyes of uneven size and shape, and the slight smudge of the pen where it formed the mouth. 'This is Balloonhead,' said Angela triumphantly. 'He is going to take on the role of, well, Balloonhead. The lead campaigner for Fuxit. Everyone say hello.' A less than enthusiastic hello came from the other toys, but Balloonhead didn't seem to mind. His empty head just bobbled around in the air, and he couldn't hear what anyone was saying anyway, as no one had bothered to draw him any ears. It meant he wasn't a good listener.

'Well,' said Rabbitman, 'now we have been introduced to Mr Balloonhead –'

'Not Mr Balloonhead,' interrupted Angela. 'Just Balloonhead.'

'I see,' continued Rabbitman. 'Well, now we have been introduced to Balloonhead, shall we continue?'

* * *

But, despite all he had achieved, sitting in the Rabbitman room in the Gold House, President Rabbitman's happiness was not complete. He had indigestion. It had been plaguing him since supper, as though a fury had hidden itself in the bottom of the third taco bowl he had devoured, and having been ingested was now tying knots in his lower bowel. Yes, that was it, the third taco bowl. He had felt fine until then. Not even Bunny sucking his cock, or a second glass of sarsaparilla, had managed to shake it loose. Rabbitman let off a loud trump of taco-laden wind, but even that didn't help. Feeling increasingly sorry for himself, Rabbitman stared into the fire and wondered whether to call the Gold House physician for a dose of salts. But as he stared into the fire, Rabbitman couldn't help noticing the way one of the larger logs was burning. It looked almost like a face in the flames. More than that, a screaming face, and a familiar face. As Rabbitman leaned forward in disbelief, he found himself saying a name out loud, a name he thought he had long forgotten: 'Balloonhead?' As the name came from Rabbitman's lips, the burning face seemed to open its incandescent eyes and stare right back at him. Rabbitman looked on in horror as it seemed to open wide its fiery mouth to shout at him, to call out his name, and then ever wider, to swallow him.

Rabbitman jumped back into his chair, stopped only by the back rest, and almost sent himself and the chair toppling over. The shock was enough to release the full power of the fury that had seized his guts, and at the moment he hit the chair back, Rabbitman let out an almighty fart, loud enough to shake the window panes, and noxious enough to fill the air with what could best be described as a sulphurous fug of semi-gaseous bodily discharge. As the fart drove all clean air fleeing from the room, the door opened and a smart young buck, with greased black hair, and dressed in an excessively smart black suit, entered. The young buck struggled for a moment to control his natural urge to gag at the smell Rabbitman had let rip, but being a well-trained professional, soon found himself able to say, 'Mr President, your guest has arrived.' The young buck quickly turned, as though desperate for oxygen, and left the room, closing the door firmly behind him. Rabbitman looked on with a mixture of bemusement and discomfit. The bemusement was because he was not expecting any guest. The discomfit was from the slight damp patch that had formed in the gusset of his underpants.

'Wait a minute!' cried Rabbitman after the young buck had left, rousing himself in the process from both the disturbing vision in the fire and the astonishing fart. Anger rose in him too as he realised one of his underlings had dared to leave his presence without waiting for permission to go. This was unheard of behaviour in the Rabbitman Gold House. 'Wait a minute!' called Rabbitman again. 'Come back here. Come back here! What guest? I'm not expecting any guest.'

'It's no use,' said a voice from somewhere near the window. 'He's one of mine. I mean he came with me. It seemed easier than using one of your chaps. As an introduction I mean. But I'm afraid he's a bit of a novice. He's not used to all the smells an aged body like yours can emit.' The voice spoke calmly, in an old-fashioned English accent, as though wilfully oblivious to the rage burning in Rabbitman's face.

* * *

'Who's playing the intruder?' asked Big Ted.

'I had thought of you,' said Angela.

* * *

'Who the hell are you?' snarled Rabbitman, reaching for the panic button near the fire place. 'You're not allowed in here.'

'Don't you remember me Bunny Boy?' asked the voice. Rabbitman did not give his eyes time to take in the features of the intruder now seated on the corner of his desk. Had he done so he would have seen a devilishly handsome creature, clearly dressed by the same tailor who had furnished the recently departed young buck. Only the addition of a flamboyant bow tie and an intricate *art nouveau* breast pin – perhaps of silver, depicting Adam and Eve standing beneath the Tree of Knowledge, the serpent still coiled around its trunk, watching Eve handing the forbidden fruit to Adam, and Adam accepting it greedily – suggested the intruder had a higher status. Despite

Rabbitman's liking for precious trinkets, he missed all this detail as he pressed the panic button, setting off the harsh main lights in the room, and bringing in a dozen heavily-armed security guards.

Rabbitman began shouting. 'Who is this?' he said repeatedly, not looking in the direction he pointed. The security guards fanned out, expecting to find an intruder hiding under the president's desk. But no one was there.

With the order given to stand down, at last the commander dared to ask the most dangerous question of the evening. 'Who do you mean, Mr President?' he asked.

The most important rabbit in the world could barely control his anger at such an insolent question. He swore at the commander, raising his paw again to point at the intruder, but looking this time where he pointed. 'Him,' he said, almost as though it was too late to stop the word emerging from his mouth, leaving Rabbitman with only the power to turn it from a venomous snarl into a confused mumble. 'Him,' he repeated. 'He was there a minute ago. One of interns let him in.'

The commander cupped his hand to his earpiece, and the microphone strapped to the side of his head, and asked the control room for information on who had been into the Rabbitman Room that evening. But the answer came back, no one since Mrs Rabbitman several hours earlier. Certainly no one in the last hour.

Rabbitman was apoplectic. He ordered the commander and his guardsmen out of the room, almost beating them as they retreated with a copy of *The Freedonian Conservative*, snatched from a nearby side table. Alone again, he threw the magazine aimlessly away, and like a man possessed, began to search on his own for the missing intruder. Only when he had finally come to the same conclusion as the commander did the most important rabbit in the world relax. It was true, he was alone in the room. But that was not enough to save either the commander or his guardsman. Rabbitman picked up the internal telephone.

'This is the President,' he said.

'Yes, Mr President,' said the voice at the other end of the line.

'Tonight's security detail,' continued Rabbitman. 'Are they reliable?'

'I believe they have all been through SF86 vetting,' said the voice on the line. 'I believe that would be standard procedure. They are from the Sixty-Sixth Detachment. I believe they are reliable.'

'So you believe, do you!' said Rabbitman sarcastically. 'And who the fuck are you to believe anything? I want them replaced.'

'Yes, Mr President.'

'All of them,' added Rabbitman. 'And I mean immediately! Tonight'

'Yes, Mr President,' said the voice.

'Send them to the Pacific Front. Now. I want them there tonight!' shouted Rabbitman.

'Yes, Mr President,' said the voice. 'But it is Christmas. Many of them have their families in town.'

'Send them all to the Pacific front. Them and their fucking families,' shouted Rabbitman. 'And if you've a problem with that, you can go too.'

'Yes, Mr President,' said the voice. 'They will be gone within the hour.'

Rabbitman slammed down the telephone and returned to the fireplace. He picked up the glass of sarsaparilla he had been drinking while looking into the fire, and took a sip. Still holding the drink, he sat again in the fireside chair, only to stand up immediately, mumbling curses as he crossed the room to dim the lights to their original low level. Once again the firelight and the soft glow of the Louis XVI candelabras came to dominate the room, and Rabbitman returned to his chair.

'That's better,' said the voice behind him again. 'All those harsh lights are very unflattering.' Rabbitman leapt to his feet again, turning round as he did so. Once again he reached for the panic button. 'I wouldn't bother with that,' said the intruder 'You don't want to cry wolf too often. Or bear in this case.' Although Rabbitman was not in the mood to take advice from an intruder in his own home, this advice felt like an order he could not refuse. He could not say his movements were involuntary, as though someone was physically forcing his paw away from the panic button, but they were not exactly voluntary either.

'Who the hell are you?' Rabbitman spat again, shaking his paw and arm in the air, as though trying to reassert control over his body.

'Are we going to go through this again?' said the intruder. 'You really don't recognise me? Well, I suppose it has been a long time. And you are quite old now. Maybe a bit forgetful? But perhaps you'll remember this.' As he spoke the intruder held up a scrolled parchment, written in what looked like dark red ink, the theatrical script seeming to evoke a deed from a Grimm fairy tale. Or worse.

Rabbitman looked pale and put his paw out to steady himself against the chair in which he had so recently sat. 'Titivillus!' he said with more breath than voice in his speech.

'Yes,' said Titivillus smiling. 'It's me! So *bona to vada!*' Titivillus moved towards Rabbitman, arm outstretched, ready to shake Rabbitman's paw. But Rabbitman flinched and, despite being nearly eighty, pirouetted around the chair, placing it between himself and Titivillus. 'Dear, dear,' said Titivillus. 'Is that any way to greet an old friend?'

'You're no friend of mine,' replied Rabbitman, still struggling to find his voice. 'You keep away from me.'

'As you wish,' said Titivillus, turning and walking over to the presidential desk. He cast a final look behind him in Rabbitman's direction, to make sure the president was paying attention, before settling himself on the presidential chair. Had he not been so frightened at the sight of this intruder, Rabbitman might have exploded with anger at the presumption anyone else could sit on his chair. It was his throne. But on this occasion, fear trumped anger.

'What do you want?' asked Rabbitman, recovering enough to emerge from behind the fire side chair.

'I would have thought that was obvious,' replied Titivillus. 'I mean, I would have *thought* it was obvious, but I must admit, every time I turn up I always have to say it. Especially with you Freedonians. It's as though you have all watched too many movies and we have to go through the same script. Only the English are worse than you because they have no culture of their own. They ape you Freedonians. Or you Federates, whatever it is you call yourselves these days. Isn't Feds the slang term now? Anyway, to follow the script, I'm here to collect on your debt.'

'Oh God!' cried Rabbitman.

'A bit too late for that old bean,' said Titivillus. 'You forsook Him a long time ago. Do you really think He wants to know you now?'

Rabbitman fell to his knees and tried to recite the Lord's Prayer. But he wondered if Titivillus was blocking his mind, just as he had earlier blocked his attempt to press the panic button. He found he could not remember beyond the first line. 'Our Father. Who is in –,' Rabbitman mumbled, his paws clasped together and reaching skyward.

'Heaven,' called out Titivillus helpfully.

'Our Father. Who is in Heaven,' Rabbitman tried again.

'Yes, while we are still on Earth,' interrupted Titivillus, who had managed, without Rabbitman even noticing, to stand and move from the presidential chair, to kneel next to him. Titivillus whispered into one of Rabbitman's long ears. 'It's another prayer you should have remembered, Mr President. "Blessed are the poor in spirit: for theirs is the kingdom of heaven. Blessed are they that mourn: for they shall be comforted. Blessed are the meek: for they shall inherit the earth. Blessed are they who do hunger and thirst after righteousness: for they shall be filled. Blessed are the merciful: for they shall obtain mercy. Blessed are the pure in heart: for they shall see God. Blessed are the peacemakers: for they shall be called the children of God. Blessed are they who are persecuted for righteousness' sake: for theirs is the kingdom of heaven."' Titivillus stood upright. Looking down at Rabbitman he said coldly: 'Now which of those applies to you, Mr President?'

§2

'I'm going to the shop,' called Angela's mother up the stairs. 'Do you want to come?' Without a second thought, Angela was on her feet and hurtling down the stairs. The thought of some sweets, maybe a bottle of pop too, if her mother had enough money, and a return to the snow outside, was an irresistible draw.

With Angela gone for an unspecified duration, the toys looked at each other in silence, unsure what to do. 'Perhaps we should carry on without her,' suggested Nou Nou. 'We have the script.'

'I think it is very rude of her to go like that,' said Rabbitman. 'Very very rude.'

'Oh shut up Rabbitman,' said Bobbi. 'She's allowed to have fun too. This play is very dark. It's probably good to get her away from it.'

'Yes,' agreed Nou Nou. 'I'm not sure it's suitable for a little girl.'

'She wrote it,' said Big Ted.

'Exactly,' said Bobbi. 'She's seen the news and filtered the experience into something she can cope with. It's like trying to take control of an uncontrollable situation. To stop it would be to bury it. Bury all those fears. That could be worse.'

'Thank you Dr Freud,' said Rabbitman sarcastically.

'How about,' said Bobbi, ignoring Rabbitman's comment while getting to her feet. 'While Angela's away, I tell you another story?'

'I'm not sure I can cope with two stories at once,' said Big Ted ruefully. 'I think I'll get them confused.'

'Don't worry,' said Bobbi, 'this is a related story. It's set in the same world as Angela's play, but it's about another group of people. A group of people coping with life after the likes of Rabbitman have taken over. There's more to life than Rabbitman, so my story is about that "more to life". It's about some extraordinary ordinary people, and what happens to them. What do you think?'

The toys began to talk amongst themselves, debating whether to start their own story. After a while they decided to take a vote on Bobbi's proposal. Having approved the idea they gathered round Bobbi to listen. 'As I said. This is a story about people,' she began. 'Ordinary people.'

* * *

Clearly the woman was in some distress. That was not an unusual sight at the door of All Saint's Margaret Street church. Even before the general collapse of the country, the Reverend Penny Farthing had frequently answered a hammering at the door and found a destitute man or woman standing before her, asking for help. And before the general collapse of the country, the Reverend Penny Farthing had always offered help. But now it was much more difficult. Now, even people like the Reverend Penny Farthing rarely had cash in their pockets to spend, let alone give away. Although she knew what Jesus would do, the Reverend Penny Farthing often found herself keeping a few coins back for herself and her verger.

Not that anyone should think Penny was selfish, or uncaring, or unholy. Penny gave away what she could. She just had very little to give away. 'Forgive me, Lord,' she would say, 'but I cannot live like the birds of the air or the lilies of the field. That was a beautiful sermon, but not entirely practical.' Nonetheless, it came into her mind every time she apologised to a beggar and told a little white lie that she had no money to give.

Yet, that night was different in so many ways. For a start neither Penny nor the verger had any money in their pockets as they walked back to All Saint's church, along the dark streets of Fitzrovia, from their allocated Public Information Office. Their PIO was housed in the empty halls of the old British Museum, where the European League's international aid programme, EuroAid, had set up a soup kitchen. There, local people, with the right identity papers, could have a basic meal, and watch the one hour daily broadcast from the BBC on one of the few functioning television sets in the district. This usually comprised nothing more than a short news bulletin and some old cartoons, but it added a kind of structure to the otherwise dreary days of the year. And that night it had given Penny and the verger their first and only meal of the day. They had eaten it in unusual silence, for no other reason than the verger had upset Penny by earlier swapping half their store of precious candles for a case of unctuous castor oil.

'Mr Yates, I distinctly recall asking you to try to get some wine for Communion,' said Penny when the verger had returned with the castor oil.

'It was the closest I could manage, vicar,' replied the verger. 'I'm sure there's no wine in Englandshire no more. Not unless you live in one of the enclaves. The Archbishop will have wine now she's in Canterbury. But there's nothing like that round here.'

Penny knew the verger had tried his best, and perhaps replacing the sweet wine of Communion with the bitter oil of the castor bean was an appropriate sign of the times.

It was on their journey back to All Saint's church that a woman had come up the them in the street. It was a foolhardy thing to do at night. One assumed it was an attack. Perhaps that was why Penny had been so sharp, calling out before the woman got too close for her to go away. Penny knew she spoke more harshly than she intended, and as the woman dissolved into the darkness, Penny felt guilty for it. What she had said was no way for a woman of the cloth to speak. Perhaps she would have spoken more kindly had she not still felt hungry, and if she had not been so annoyed with the verger walking by her side. The meagre meal at the PIO only served to remind her she how hungry she was, rather than fill her stomach. But no. Even with a full stomach, and more kindly thoughts towards the verger, she would not have been any kinder. Kindness might have led to a mugging, assault, or even murder. You had to be forceful. Especially at night. You had to push people away. To assume the worse. You had to, even on Christmas Eve. Fear made people unkind.

There had been another time of course. A time when Christmas Eve meant three services at the church, including the children's nativity play, and midnight mass, all celebrated with real

Communion wine. Penny smiled at the thought of the old midnight mass, and, wanting to mend bridges with the verger, almost said something about it to him. Except it wasn't wise to talk while walking the streets at night. Voices just drew attention. It was better to get back to the relative safety of the church in silence. So Penny just thought about the old midnight mass. In silence she remembered how it would be filled with boisterous drunks disgorged from nearby pubs, and how the drunken mob sung carols with more gusto than talent. Penny's silent thoughts led to silent tears. It was a battle she'd fought and lost to keep those days going once Balloonhead and his cronies took over. And now there was no Christmas Eve service at all. There would be a mass on Christmas Day, early enough to give people a chance to get to church and home before the boys of the gangs woke for the day. But even then there would be few worshippers. Who could blame people for staying away? Only a fool would give thanks for the monochrome world of Englandshire.

Reaching Tottenham Court Road, Penny and the verger stopped outside the building that had once been Heal's. Standing on one of the few lit streets left in the city, and one with its own armed guard, the verger dared at last to speak. 'Rabbitman's going to turn it into a casino,' he said, trying to make amends with Penny by focusing on a common enemy.

'What into a casino?' Penny asked.

The verger pointed at the old Heal's building. 'This whole street is going to become a new enclave. Just for tourists. Sex tourists and gamblers.'

'I suppose it's a kind of gentrification,' said Penny with black humour. 'Perhaps we should protest.'

'They just shoot protestors round here, vicar,' said the verger, not picking up on Penny's irony.

'We'll also have to register at a new PIO,' continued Penny. 'That won't be easy. They won't let us cross the enclave when it's finished.'

'But you're a vicar, vicar,' said the verger. 'They'll have to let you cross.'

'Do you really think they'll want a vicar outside their brothels and casinos, Mr Yates? Unless it's tarts and vicars night.'

The two of them moved to the edge of the pavement, stopping at the curb to look up and down the long and empty street before crossing. It was an old habit, to follow an irrelevant Green Cross Code, drummed into them decades earlier by Alvin Stardust and the Tufty Club, even though the likelihood of encountering a moving vehicle in London these days was very slim. In one direction, in the distance, a burned-out Boris bus, lying on its side, could be seen outside Centre Point. But in the other, a more unusual sight met their eyes. A car was moving. It drove slowly down the street towards them. 'He's going the wrong way, vicar,' said the verger. 'This is a one-way street.'

Penny did not respond. As the car drew near they could see it was an armoured vehicle, in dark military green, but looking almost black under the yellow glow of the military flood lamps illuminating the street. It stopped beside them and a Freedonian voice called out: 'This area is off limits.' Both Penny and the verger had enough sense to keep their identity cards and permits in their hands when walking outside. Reaching into a coat pocket to retrieve anything after being stopped by a militiaman was asking to be shot.

'We have permission,' said Penny coldly.

'That's right,' added the verger. 'We have permission.'

The militiaman got out of the armoured car and took their papers. He looked at the identity cards closely, pointing the beam of his long handled torch, that could easily have doubled as a truncheon, into the vicar's face to match her to the photograph on her card. He then moved on to the verger. Eventually the militiaman said, 'They seem to be in order, but don't hang around too long. We're expecting some German businessmen, and their detail might not ask before shooting.' It was a blunt but real warning.

'You're with the Rabbitman Guard?' asked Penny, unsure why she wanted to engage the sour mercenary in conversation.

'Yeah. What of it?' said the militiaman.

'And the Germans will be going to the brothel at Goodge Street station?' asked Penny.

'You mean the Pluto Club? That's right,' said the militiaman.

'But it's Christmas, officer,' said Penny, trying to flatter the militiaman with an elevated obeisance. 'Doesn't everyone need a night off from –' Penny paused, trying to find a neutral word to describe the forced labour of the sex slaves held in carriages, converted into themed brothel cars, parked on the old underground platforms, deep beneath their feet. But there wasn't one.

'Fuck that, lady,' said the militiaman, a ball of malice forming at the back of his throat like a globule of phlegm. 'It's Christmas Eve so they'll be fucked all night.' He laughed as he added, 'They're easy meat and a good buy, so they'll be fucked well into Christmas day.'

The verger stepped forward, saying, 'That's no way to talk to a vicar.'

'Screw you, old man,' sneered the militiaman hitting the verger with the end of his torch, sending the verger to the ground. The militiaman reached inside his belted coat for his pistol, suggesting a final end to this conversation, but he stopped as Penny knelt down, placing herself between him and the verger.

'This man and I,' shouted Penny, 'are under the direct protection of the Archbishop of Canterbury.'

'Screw your archbishop,' said the militiaman.

'Do you want to explain to your captain why you've disobeyed orders?' Penny shouted again. She sounded convincing, but was unsure whether the Rabbitman Guard had ever been party to a supposed agreement to allow the clergy, outside the enclaves, to go unhindered by the militia gangs.

Had he been in the mood to admit it, the militiaman might have said he didn't know anything about an agreement. But fear of his commanding officer made him err on the side of caution. 'Fuck off out of here,' he spat, getting back into his armoured car. He felt humiliated by the woman in a dog collar, and the stupid old man with her, and wanted to strike back. 'Fuck off out of here, while we fuck those hoes. We'll show them a real good time tonight. I promise. You've put me in the mood for it.' Driving off he shouted. 'We'll make them lie back and think of England.'

§3

Back from her trip to the shop, now armed with a bag of Hula Hoops and a bottle of Bing, Angela sat with the toys and pondered which of them should play her next character.

'Is it such a difficult choice?' asked Bobbi, wondering if she might be lined up for a part.

'Not usually,' said Angela, 'but in this case it has to be someone with hands instead of paws.' Bobbi tried to hide her disappointment. 'It won't make sense if they have paws,' added Angela.

As she spoke, Angela reached over the soft toys and picked up a gaudy string puppet. It was dressed in bulbous stripy pantaloons, its face painted white, with two tiny black balls as its eyes, a large red ball forming its nose, and a thin painted crescent line marking its smiling, but lipless, mouth. Its gangly arms and oversized boots were caught up in its strings, but Angela soon untangled them, and holding the marionette by the wooden crossbar, made it dance. This was Floppy the Clown, or Mr Floppy as Angela liked to call him.

'My Floppy,' said Angela, 'I have a very important role for you.' Mr Floppy looked pleased. 'You are going to play the lead in a side story. I will need you and Yellow Bear.' Angela leaned over and picked up a bright yellow bear, well-loved, but the victim of some very hard times. Its head had been detached from its body, and re-sewn back, numerous times, although rarely with yellow thread.

'Fantastic darling,' said Mr Floppy. 'I'm going to star in my own show at last.'

'Co-star,' Yellow Bear corrected him. 'I'm in it too.'

'Yes,' said Mr Floppy, 'but there are stars and there are co-stars. You be a co-star if you want to. I'm going to be the star!'

Angela coughed to regain their attention and began the performance. 'Mr Floppy,' said Angela, 'you can stay as Mr Floppy, and Yellow Bear, you are going to play a doctor. Let's call her Dr Timoria.'

* * *

When Mr Floppy awoke from troubling dreams he was confused.

Although nominally a grown man, Mr Floppy still liked to stay with his parents, or rather with Mummy, in their chocolate-box mansion on the south side of the Canterbury Enclave in southern Englandshire. There Mummy's maid cooked, and cleaned, and cared for Mr Floppy, like any other servant, but Mummy herself gave him a special kind of love only a Mummy could give her boy. In his own apartment in Freedonia, or his private rooms at the Gold House, Mr Floppy might replicate any of the cooking, and cleaning, and general care, with just a few dollars paid to an illegal migrant, as he invariably did. But it would take more than just a few dollars to replicate the special care that Mummy gave him.

And Daddy?

Well, Mr Floppy had two daddies now, both of whom provided what he wanted most from them: money. There was Bio-Dad, a somewhat diminished figure in Mr Floppy's eyes, but worth keeping on side for the inheritance he would no doubt leave, not soon enough, to his biological spawn. And then there was Freedonian Daddy, not only very rich, but very powerful. Very, very powerful. Freedonian Daddy happened to be the leader of Freedonia, President Rabbitman. 'Yes, Rabbitman's an immoral bastard,' Mr Floppy once admitted to news reader Kate Oldman. 'But with his views on muslims, blacks, yids, wops, faggots, and most of all the bitch-dykes, all of whom are dragging down the country with their victim culture, he's very entertaining.' Of course Oldman challenged Mr Floppy's foul language, but Mr Floppy just tweeted live on air that Oldman is yet another bitch-dyke without a sense of humour. 'It's just a joke: get a sense of humour!' he tweeted.

But this morning Mr Floppy woke up confused. He knew he had gone to bed as usual, in his parents' house. But the last really clear thing he could remember was Mummy closing the door behind her as she left his bedroom, having delivered a cup of warm cocoa to help him sleep. After that, the memories were more hazy. He was pretty sure he had drunk the cocoa. And that he had turned off the bedside lamp. And that he had placed his left hand into his pants, searching for his tiny cock, so embarrassingly shrivelled it had earned him the nickname *Choady* at school. He was pretty sure too he had followed the usual routine, in the darkness, of imagining Mummy fucking Freedonian Daddy while he masturbated his little worm. He seemed to remember that worm then giving up its tiny dribble of watery sperm. He was certain, in fact, it had been a typical night at home.

But this morning Mr Floppy woke up confused. He was not in his bed anymore. He was not in his bedroom. He was not in his parents' house in the Canterbury Enclave. He was not in the Gold House. He was not anywhere he recognised. He wasn't even in a bed. Not a real bed. He seemed to be lying on a kind of padded trolley, at least judging from what little he could see and feel, his freedom of movement being severely restricted by a series of thick straps holding him firmly down. As for the room, it was painted throughout in a stern battleship grey, the sinister colour only enhanced by what seemed to be no more than an forty watt incandescent light bulb, hanging from a twisted cord in the centre of the ceiling. Wherever Mr Floppy was it was a grim place.

'Good morning Mr Floppy,' said a woman's voice entering through a door just out of sight to Mr Floppy's left. 'I trust you slept well.'

'Where am I?' asked Mr Floppy, half expecting to be told there had been an accident. Perhaps a gas leak at the house, an explosion, or something to explain why he was no longer in his own bed, but strapped to a trolley. 'Am I hurt?' he added, touting for some words of comfort. 'Did my parents survive?'

'Survive?' asked the woman. 'Survive what, Mr Floppy?'

'The gas explosion,' said Mr Floppy, the thought of his inheritance starting to permeate his mind.

The woman laughed gently. 'Oh I see,' she said. 'You are trying to understand your situation.

You imagine there must have been a gas explosion, or something that has brought you to this hospital.

'So I am in a hospital?' said Mr Floppy.

'Very good, Mr Floppy. In less than three minutes you have managed to get out of me some cogent information. I see you are as manipulative as your reputation suggests. If only you could have put that skill towards something socially useful you might have been a real journalist. And you wouldn't be here now of course.'

'I am a real journalist,' said Mr Floppy defiantly, but the woman just laughed.

'If that helps you sleep at night, Mr Floppy. Although I hear you have other methods.'

The woman came into view. Or partially into view. She stood between Mr Floppy's line of sight and the bare lightbulb so her face was in deep shadow while the light from the bulb formed what looked to Mr Floppy like a halo around her head as it refracted through her yellow fur. 'My name is Dr Timoria,' said the floppy-headed bear standing in front of him. 'And I am going to take care of you.'

'What is wrong with me?' asked Mr Floppy, immediately regretting the open ended question as the yellow bear laughed again.

'I'm afraid, Mr Floppy, it would take a long time to answer that question,' she said. 'But rest assured you are in good hands.'

'Where am I?' asked Mr Floppy again, adding this time, 'and where is my mother?' Dr Timoria did not answer this time. Instead she seemed to be conducting a physical examination of Mr Floppy's naked body, more in the manner of a pathologist, Mr Floppy thought, than a healer of the sick.

'You seem to be in good physical shape, Mr Floppy,' the yellow bear said eventually. 'But the body and mind are linked, so if we are going to cure your mind, we must do so though your body.'

'There's nothing wrong with my mind,' said Mr Floppy, again with a sense of defiance. He strained to sit up, but the straps holding him down allowed no movement.

'I'm afraid there is, Mr Floppy,' said the bear quietly. 'Or you wouldn't be here, would you?'

Doctor Timoria left the room, but with the door still ajar Mr Floppy could hear her talking, possibly to a nurse, telling her his was a serious case. He heard the doctor say the words, 'Definitely a case of chronic imbecility. The man is a moron, so it will be the full treatment.' Mr Floppy heard the doctor say something about his treatment lasting years. And then about cut backs. He thought it was like listening to a whingeing junior doctor in the days of the NHS, moaning about cuts in funding. He thought he was getting the measure of Dr Timoria.

As Dr Timoria returned to the room she stopped in the doorway and called back to the nurse outside, 'And could you get me an Article Fifty Notice? Then I'll need you to act as witness.' Turning again, the doctor walked to the side of Mr Floppy's bed, and for the first time Mr Floppy could see her white coat was covered in what looked like brown mud. Except he knew it was dried blood. He could smell her too. In the enclaves no doctor would smell of body odour. No one in the enclaves smelled of BO at all. Not usually. Maybe for a short while, after a game of squash, or a heavy night out on the town. But never a doctor in a clinic.

'I am not in the enclave any more,' said Mr Floppy, his heart sinking at the thought.

'No,' said the doctor distractedly, not bothering to look up from the clipboard on which she was writing copious notes.

'How did I get here?' asked Mr Floppy, but the doctor did not bother to answer. 'Was I kidnapped?' But again the yellow bear did not answer, although this time she did not have to. Almost as soon as Mr Floppy uttered the word kidnapped, a terrible cry could be heard from somewhere outside. A nurse ran into Mr Floppy's room.

'It's the editor of the *Mail*, doctor,' said the nurse. 'He's making a terrible fuss.'

'Such a cry baby!' said the doctor, sighing deeply as she spoke. 'Alright, slap him a few times across the face, and see if that calms him down. Slap him hard mind you. Gentle slaps won't do the trick. The harder the better. If that doesn't work give him one hundred cc's of *voguel aether.* Then prep him for the leucotomy. I thought I had explained to him it is for his own good. To stop all those nasty little paranoid thoughts about scroungers, traitors and foreigners. I said to him we'll all feel much better afterwards.' The nurse turned to leave the room, only to be stopped by the doctor calling her back, 'And Hadiza, can you see where Vashti has got to? I need her to witness an Article Fifty Notice.' With her instructions the nurse left the room, closing the door behind her.

'Now where was I, Mr Floppy?' continued the doctor, lowering her clipboard and looking at her patient.

'Was all that staged to try and frighten me?' asked Mr Floppy. 'You expect me to believe you are about to perform a lobotomy on the editor of the *Mail?*'

'Don't be silly,' replied Dr Timoria. 'That would be ridiculous. A simple procedure like a lobotomy can be done by one of the nurses. Hadiza and Vashti can quite easily wield a knife. Even an orderly could do it. And I would ask you not to use the word lobotomy. It's considered rather offensive these days. But, in answer to your question, no it was not staged to frighten you, and yes, the editor of the *Mail* is in the next room, awaiting treatment, and acting like a big baby because of it. I hope we are not going to have any of that stuff and nonsense from you Mr Floppy. This is Englandshire after all. We expect men to have a bit more backbone here.'

'You haven't explained why I am here. What do you want of me?' asked Mr Floppy. 'Why am I being held here? I insist you let me go.'

'You are being held here for the good of society,' said the yellow bear, looking again at her clipboard, but this time turning the pages. 'Blood pressure is a little high. Any history of high blood pressure in the family?' she asked. Mr Floppy struggled, as though trying to sit up, but still the straps held him tight. 'I'll take that as a no,' murmured the bear. 'Otherwise it tends to complicate things. Best to keep them simple, even if it's not true.'

At that moment Nurse Vashti entered the room. 'Sorry Dr Timoria,' she said. 'We'd run out of Article Fifty Notices, so I had to go down to Central Stores.'

'Did you bring some spare?' asked the doctor.

'I brought a hundred,' answered Nurse Vashti.

'We'll need double that to see out the week,' said Dr Timoria. 'Get some more when you have a mo'. Let's just get this one all legal.' Dr Timoria then turned to Mr Floppy and reading from the top paper on her clipboard said: 'Floppy the Clown, having failed to attend mandatory appointments for social reintegration, you are hereby detained under Article Fifty of the Sociopathic Care Act 2018, on the grounds of your potential danger to society.'

'No!' shouted Mr Floppy, his struggles now strong enough to shake the trolley to which he was strapped, although showing little sign of loosening the ties that bound him. 'No,' Mr Floppy repeated.

'No, no, no! That's not what the Act was for! It's not for people like me.'

'A review of this detention will take place at the end of twenty-eight days, as required under the Act,' continued Dr Timoria, signing a sheet of paper from which she read, and handing it to Nurse Vashti to countersign. 'When you've signed it file it with the others.' Nurse Vashti then left the room, closing the door behind her.

Mr Floppy seemed calm now, but his muscles were still tense. He was crying silently, unable to wipe his eyes except by closing them tightly, hoping each time he opened them again he would wake up from his nightmare. Dr Timoria took a tissue from her blood-stained pocket and wiped his eyes. 'There, there,' she said. 'It's good to cry. Even if it is only for yourself. But you know you are very sick. And we are going to make you better.'

'I'm not sick,' insisted Mr Floppy, almost pleading for the doctor to believe him.

'I know,' said Dr Timoria. 'It can seem that way. It can seem as if we are going about our business as usual, and we are fine, but inside there is something wrong. Something seriously wrong. And when it's pointed out to us we don't believe it. We think, but I'm fine. But we are not fine are we, Mr Floppy? We are anything but fine. And you have not been fine for a very long time. Deep down, you know that is true, don't you, Mr Floppy. Deep, deep down, you know you are an imbecile, and as an imbecile you are a danger to society. So what we need to do is dig down, beyond that imbecile you, until we reveal the healthy you. The real you. I know you will protest. Everyone protests when they come here. At first anyway. But we both know what I'm telling you is true. Despite what you say, I know you want me to cut out the unhealthy you, like chopping away weeds in an unkept garden. That way we'll leave the real you enough space in which to bloom again.'

Dr Timoria was talking in a whisper as she ended her monologue, but Mr Floppy was unsure if what she said was meant really to comfort him, or as a softly spoken threat. 'But I'm not sick,' Mr

Floppy said again, echoing the doctor's quiet tone of voice.

'That's only the weeds in the garden talking,' said the doctor softly. 'And we are going to cut them away.'

The doctor stood up abruptly, and walked to the side of the room, out of Mr Floppy's line of sight. Mr Floppy could hear her arranging what sounded like medicine bottles, or something, on a metal surface.

'And you know, Mr Floppy, it's exactly that kind of defiance that brought you here in the first place,' said Dr Timoria, loudly this time, echoing the unsympathetic tone she had used when talking about the editor of the *Mail*. 'You have been told you are sick on many occasions. You can hardly forget them. You were told it on that tour of Freedonian universities you did, when there were all those student protests. What did you call it? *The Gormless Twassock Tour.* And you were told it when you said transexuals are mentally ill. That black people shouldn't complain when they're shot by the police. I think you said they wouldn't be shot if they weren't up to something. And then you said ugly dykes should stop complaining about men and welcome what they really want. What was it you said that time? "An injection of man meat." And you were told you were sick when you claimed rape is a myth. And when you said muslims are all born murderers. So many times you were told. So you must see you are sick. Or rather, I must help you to see you are sick. That's why I am here, Mr Floppy: to cure you of the delusion you are normal. I am a doctor after all.'

This time is was Mr Floppy's turn to laugh, although it sounded more like hysteria. 'I see. I get it. You're a bleeding-heart liberal. Probably one of those feminist dyke-bitches. Is that why you always stand with your back to the light? Too ugly to let me see you?'

Dr Timoria moved to the side of the trolley onto which Mr Floppy was strapped. He could see her reach down to the side of it, but unseen from him she stretched underneath and pulled a handle. As she did, the trolley seemed to collapse under Mr Floppy, and he screamed out in pain as his back arched unsupported before crashing down onto the trolley again. He was now sitting up, or partially up as though in a dentist chair. 'It's alright, Mr Floppy,' said the doctor with excessive politeness. 'I don't mind you seeing me properly. I hope that's better. But you really should stop criticising how other people look. You are somewhat boss-eyed yourself, you know, and you have lips like a trout. You're hardly an oil painting.'

'Fuck off!' shouted Mr Floppy, his highly developed sense of vanity wounded by a mere doctor daring to criticise his looks. But Dr Timoria just kicked the trolley with the side of her boot, sending another painful jolt into Mr Floppy's body.

'I see it's time to start your treatment,' said the doctor, moving again to the side of the room to count bottles, but returning quickly this time pushing a brushed steel trolly on which Mr Floppy could see a series of small phials and some boxes with medical labels on them. And then there was an array of tools. There were four or five syringes, some scalpels and other medical instruments, and what looked like a small pair of pliers, or perhaps they were bolt cutters. 'Tell me, Mr Floppy, are you familiar with the concept of chemical castration?'

Mr Floppy felt his stomach churn for a moment as he eyed the bolt cutters. 'What do you mean?' he asked.

'It's a perfectly simple question,' said the doctor. 'Chemical castration – you are familiar with the concept?'

Despite the fear mounting in his body, Mr Floppy felt his only option was to sound bullish. 'You do know what they will do to you, if you hurt me?' he said, trying to keep his voice calm to appear convincing.

'They?' asked the doctor.

'You do know who I am?' asked Mr Floppy, answering himself, 'I am the personal friend of the President of Freedonia. A *personal* friend,' he emphasised. 'I'm talking about President Rabbitman. What do you think he will do when he hears how you are treating me here?'

'Very little I suspect,' said the doctor calmly, whilst reordering the phials and boxes on the trolley.

'Wrong!' said Mr Floppy triumphantly. 'He'll make you wish you were dead.'

'I felt that way the moment he was elected,' said the doctor dryly. 'But what I meant was, very little in time I suspect.'

Mr Floppy went pale. He realised he must be in the hands of fanatics. Terrorists, intent on making an example of him. They probably expected to die in the name of their cause, these remnants of the liberal underground who called themselves the Silent Majority. Whatever retribution happened to them, they expected to die, so threats were no use. He might be a personal friend of Rabbitman, but no one in the Gold House was about to send in the marines to save him. No one even knew he was there. Later they might bomb hell out of this place, but Mr Floppy knew it would be too late. By then he would be long dead, hacked to pieces by Dr Crippin here.

'My question was,' continued the doctor, now in the manner of a stern school mistress wondering why a recalcitrant school boy was failing to answer a very simple question. 'Are you familiar with chemical castration?'

'So that's the great liberal utopia is it?' said Mr Floppy, trying to sound even more brazen. 'Kidnap a Jewish boy in the middle of the night, and threaten him with medical experiments. What kind of social liberal does that make you? Dr Mengele?'

The doctor laughed again. Longer and louder this time. 'I'm afraid you are very much mistaken, Mr Floppy,' she said, 'if you think I am a liberal. Your kind killed off the liberals. Don't you remember?'

'What do you mean, my kind?' parried Mr Floppy, trying to gain the moral high ground.

Dr Timoria laughed again. 'I was wondering if you'd try that trick,' she said. 'It's an old one of yours. From the days when we had a free press. I'm glad to see you haven't forgotten it. Someone dares to challenge you, or contradict you, or stop you, and you try to wrong foot them by hiding behind your supposed ethnicity. What did you used to call it? Ah yes, "Reverse Victimhood". It used to work when the country was run by decent people. It wrong footed them big time. You'd attack women, and blacks, and gays, and muslims, and sometimes even Jews, and when you were called out for it you'd say, "So this is how a liberal society treats a little Jewish boy?" You'd call people hypocrites and they'd be cowed by your accusation in case their friends thought they were being racist. Or homophobic. Or something illiberal. It used to work back then, didn't it? But now? Well, now the trouble is, Mr Floppy, we know the truth, don't we?'

'What you mean?' said Mr Floppy.

'You know what I mean,' said Dr Timoria. 'The truth that you are not Jewish. It's all a lie.'

'What are you talking about?' said Mr Floppy, sounding genuinely confused.

'It's a lie,' repeated Doctor Timoria. 'It was just a way of wrong-footing the liberals. It was a way of playing on their innate sense of guilt. As you know, all liberals feel guilty. It's what defines them, and it's their achilles heel. In fact it's the first line of any *Liberal Manifesto*, "Sorry everyone, I shouldn't have done that." But in the end it's their downfall, as they try to be nice to everyone, whether they deserve it or not. And it meant they even tried to be nice to you, when you pretended to be Jewish as cover for your attacks on Jews, and blacks, and gays, and muslims, and anyone else you felt like kicking. I must admit it was a very clever ruse. But now the lie of it is all here, on this website, for anyone to see if they want to. It's the truth about you. About how you pretended to be Jewish to fend off any liberal who dared challenge your nasty little views.'

'What the fuck's a web site?' asked Mr Floppy. 'Anyway, it's not true. I am Jewish.'

'No, no, no,' said the doctor. 'The facts speak for themselves. It says here you made it all up. You can deny it of course, but why should I believe you, a diagnosed imbecile strapped to a hospital bed, when I can believe the published words on a website, and one that has been viewed by over thirty million people in the last twenty-four hours? I will go with the majority I think.'

'This is crazy,' shouted Mr Floppy. 'I am Jewish!'

'I don't think so, Mr Floppy,' insisted the doctor. 'Otherwise why would you say so many unpleasant things about Jews? It doesn't really add up does it? An anti-semitic Jew? Ridiculous!'

'I have only spoken against whingeing liberal Jews, who spend one minute moaning about anti-semitism and the next about Israel's treatment of the arabs,' replied Mr Floppy, trying to defend himself. 'All abuse is legitimate abuse against your enemies.'

'I'll take that lesson on board, Mr Floppy,' said the doctor. 'But if you are Jewish why have you never been circumcised? Or do you want to claim your foreskin grew back?'

'It's because, they couldn't –' said Mr Floppy. 'I mean, they couldn't.' He stopped again. Quietly he tried to explain, 'When I was due to be circumcised the rabbi told my parents he couldn't do it. He said my penis was too small. He said if he took away the foreskin there wouldn't be anything left of it.'

'Is that really the best story you could come up with?' retorted the doctor. 'I know it's a very small dick, but that fable really doesn't sound likely.'

'It's true,' insisted Mr Floppy, his voice almost turning to a whinge.

'Well, even if it is,' said the doctor, 'we are not interested in the truth any more. We live in a post-truth age now. But to return to my original question, are you familiar with chemical castration? I am going to assume that you are as I am fed up with asking. It's the process of taking away the urges some very sick men have to commit very sick crimes. We take away the physical means for those men to exercise those urges. Well, medicine has moved on since chemical castration was first used, so we doctors can now extend that concept a little.'

'You cannot do this,' said Mr Floppy, more to himself than the doctor now sitting next to him and holding the pair of bolt cutters.

'You are very sick, Mr Floppy,' continued the doctor. 'You are an imbecile and your urges are to write really very nasty things. And so, in a way, we are going to castrate you. Not your dick of course. That wouldn't make sense and it's hardly worth chopping off. Besides you don't write with your dick. At least I don't think you do. You write with your fingers. I have talked to my colleagues here in the hospital and there is promising research in the field of selective chemical limb amputation, which will one day negate the need for physical surgery. Unfortunately, budget cuts mean research in that area is not yet complete, so we are going to have to use the old-fashioned method.'

As she finished her sentence the doctor picked up a syringe, filled it from one of the glass phials on the trolley and began injecting Mr Floppy's left hand. Mr Floppy felt his fingers go numb. The doctor moved to his right side and repeated the injections on his right hand.

'As I said, Mr Floppy, chemical amputation is not yet an option, but this will work just as well. The old ways are sometimes the best, as they say, and it will stop your ability to write down your nasty little thoughts.' With that the doctor waved the bolt cutters theatrically in the air and cut off the fingers from both of Mr Floppy's hands, releasing the cords that bound him to the wooden crossbar.

When Dr Timoria had finished she began bandaging up Mr Floppy's wounds and called Nurse Vashti back into the room. 'Can you finish bandaging Mr Floppy's hands, Vashti?' she said. 'And then schedule him in for another session tomorrow. I think we will get to work on that tongue of his. It says some pretty nasty things too. But I think we can cure that quite easily.'

§4

In the Gold House Rabbitman was still kneeling on the floor trying to remember the Lord's Prayer. When even he had the intelligence to realise the words would not come, he fell onto all fours, and stayed there a full five minutes in silence, like a dumb and beaten ass cowed into submission. Except in his own mind he was not dumb, and not beaten. He was smart. He kept telling himself he knew the Lord's Prayer, and of course he would have been able to recite it, and have obtained salvation from God, if only Titivillus hadn't worked some kind of black magic voodoo on him, blocking the words from his mind and mouth. That's what he would tell people afterwards anyway.

While he was in this position Rabbitman realised the toupée had fallen from his head. The sight of it lying on the floor, like a dead ferret, roused in him a desire to return to a more human stance, and grabbing the arm of a nearby chair, he slowly raised himself to his feet. Once upright,

Rabbitman turned to face away from Titivillus and began to straighten his crumpled suit. He brushed the front panels, pulled at the arms, and ended this show of camp theatrics by adjusting his tie, assuming Titivillus was watching him closely throughout. In fact Titivillus did watch Rabbitman, and with genuine curiosity, wondering as he did so whether Rabbitman would try to save his own dignity by abandoning the toupée, still languishing on the floor. The answer was not long in coming. Rabbitman's sartorial adjustments completed, he bent down, picked up his toupée, brushed it with the palm of his hand, as though dusting a hat, and walked across the room to stand in front of a large mirror. There he returned the poor dead creature to his head, and proceeded to twist it into what seemed, to Rabbitman, a normal position. Usually Rabbitman had the services of a perruquier to help him with this, so the experience of doing such an essential, but menial, task himself was irksome. It was also more difficult than he ever imagined, which explained why the toupée was now set back to front. The full performance complete, Rabbitman turned to Titivillus and said calmly: 'May I see the contract?'

'See it?' asked Titivillus, 'Of course, but we're not going to have another movie scene are we? The one where the debtor pleads for his life in some celestial court room.'

'I don't see why not,' replied Rabbitman, taking the parchment from Titivillus. 'I don't see I have anything to lose stringing the process out. The smart thing would be to make it last as long as possible. The longer the better. You know I have enough lawyers to make this case go on for a very long time.'

Titivillus laughed. 'As long as eternity, Bunny Boy?'

'As long as eternity. Yes, that's right,' sneered Rabbitman. 'And it's Mr President to you!' Rabbitman had hoped to intimidate Titivillus by insisting on the use of his title, but instead Titivillus unnerved Rabbitman with an icy stare that sent a shiver down his spine.

Titivillus looked up at the clock and said, 'Yes, I suppose it is still Mr President. But not to me. To everyone else, maybe. But not to me, Bunny Boy. Never to me.'

For a moment Rabbitman lost his composure once again, but it returned more quickly this time as he said: 'Look, I'm sure there's a way round this. You want to take me, but there are plenty of others who could go in my place. I don't see why it matters if you take me or someone else. It's just another body for the furnace, after all.'

'Furnace?' asked Titivillus. 'Oh I see. When you put it like that, I suppose you are right. One body in a furnace is very much like another. But we don't really think of it in those terms.'

'Perhaps you should,' said Rabbitman. 'Look, I'm a businessman. A smart businessman. I know about business. Business is about units. Buying units. Making units. Shipping units. Selling units. All units. You see, you should think of bodies as units. One unit is very much like another, as long as it is a unit. What matters is the number of units. So, my body is just a unit. It's like any other unit, and as long as you reach your target, let's say a

82

thousand units a day, what does it matter what units make up that target? It's that kind of thinking that has made me so smart. Never think of individual people or things: just think of units. Everything is about units.'

'That does sound very smart,' agreed Titivillus. 'So in a sense, there are no people. No individuals, I mean. They are all just units.'

'That's it!' exclaimed Rabbitman. 'There are no people, only units. There are no things being made by people, only units made by units. Even money is just units, and you either have a lot of units or you have very few units.'

'But wouldn't that just make you a unit?' asked Titivillus. 'Like you said, your body could just be replaced by another body. Another unit that is. So why should I make a deal with you? Shouldn't I just chuck you in the furnace, as you put it, and say next?'

A brief wave of unease washed over Rabbitman's face. 'Ah, no,' he said. 'There's a difference. They are units. But I'm not a unit because I control the units. I control them because

I'm smart enough to understand they are all units. Of course, it's true, my body is a kind of unit, but I'm smart you see. Too smart just to be a unit. I have a mind as well.'

'Yes, I see it!' exclaimed Titivillus, sounding unexpectedly excited. 'In a way you are separating your mind and body. Body and soul as it were. Except, of course, that might be construed as a kind of theological heresy. I mean, isn't it a kind of Albigensianist dualism?'

'A what?' asked Rabbitman, baffled.

'Let me put it another way,' said Titivillus. 'Being so smart, you are not just a unit. So one might almost say, without wanting to sound too grand about it, that you are a kind of god. Unlike the other units you see things as they really are, and that makes you different. It stops you being just a unit because you can – how can I put it? – stand outside the system. *Deus ex machina.*'

'Yes!' exclaimed Rabbitman. 'Yes! I'm not a unit because I see things as they really are. Because I'm smart. And that does make me a kind of god.' As Rabbitman said these words there was a disturbing rattle at the window, as though the branch of a tree was rapping at the glass pane, even though no trees grew that close to the Gold House. But Rabbitman didn't notice. 'Yes, that's it,' he was still saying. 'If you're smart enough to control the units you're not a unit. You're a god.'

Titivillus had moved to the rattling window, and seemed to be staring intently at something outside, almost as though receiving new instructions. He turned to Rabbitman, and said, 'The trouble is, Bunny Boy, you signed the contract. It has your name on it. So I don't see how we can take another unit instead of you. If you see what I mean.'

'But that's my point,' said Rabbitman moving towards Titivillus. He placed his hand on Titivillus's back and led him towards the fire. 'You see, I'm too smart. Like I say, I'm not a unit. I can move units around, get them to do what I want, buy them and spend them. Whatever I want. So how about we do a new deal. How about instead of me, you take ten units. Ten souls for the price of one. That's a good rate of return.'

'Ten?' said Titivillus feigning interest. 'Why not a hundred?'

'A hundred!' said Rabbitman. 'Yes, why not a hundred.'

'Or a thousand?' suggested Titivillus.

'That's a hard bargain,' said Rabbitman. 'But I'm worth it, so yes a thousand. Even a million.'

'A million?' asked Titivillus.

'Yes, a million units,' agreed Rabbitman in a state of excitement. 'Take a million units in place of me. Or even a whole state. You could take the Pacific Coast. I wouldn't miss it. Take it, if that's enough to balance me.'

'It would make you a very weighty man,' said Titivillus. 'It's a tempting offer, but what about a different deal? How about just one unit in place of you?'

'You're a lousy businessman,' scoffed Rabbitman. 'But sure, one unit! Who do you have in mind.'

'Someone in this building,' said Titivillus.

'Anyone,' agreed Rabbitman, 'Just name them and they are yours.'

'Anyone?' asked Titivillus.

'Anyone,' repeated Rabbitman. 'How about Bunny?' asked Titivillus.

'Bunny?' said Rabbitman, his voice faltering slightly. 'No, I didn't mean Bunny. Anyone else.'

'But you said anyone,' said Titivillus insistently.

'But I didn't mean Bunny,' said Rabbitman. 'In fact, I explicitly said anyone except Bunny. I remember saying it, just now.'

'She is the perfect substitute,' said Titivillus.

'But she's my wife,' said Rabbitman. As he spoke he wondered whether this was a reason for or against.

'And she's your daughter,' said Titivillus. 'It was a deft change in the marriage law that one. Who thought you would get it through parliament so easily.'

'That proves how smart I am you see,' said Rabbitman. 'But you can't take Bunny. I couldn't live without her.'

'On the contrary,' replied Titivillus. 'You might live without her. But there's just one condition. She would have to come willingly to replace you. We couldn't just take her.'

'Why not?' asked Rabbitman, his scruples at the prospect of losing Bunny starting to wane. 'Isn't she a sinner too?'

'She is, and she will pay for her own sins. But you cannot make her pay for yours,' said Titivillus sternly. 'It must be a free choice. No coercion. That's our rules.'

'What sort of hell are you running down there?' exclaimed Rabbitman. 'I thought it was built on coercion! Anyway, women can't exercise freedom of choice. They can't cope with it.'

'You mean you don't think she will agree?' asked Titivillus.

'Bunny will do anything for me,' replied Rabbitman. 'Anything.'

§5

'What are you doing up there?' called Angela's mother up the stairs. 'You're very quiet.'

'I'm busy!' shouted Angela back, giving her mother a foretaste of Angela's rapidly approaching teenage years.

'Well, come and help me tidy up,' called Angela's mother back. 'I'm not a skivvy...' Angela's mother's voice trailed off as she returned to the kitchen, leaving Angela to sigh at being dragged away from her performance once again, mumbling that it was not fair, as she tossed Rabbitman unceremoniously on the floor, stood up, and stomped loudly down the stairs.

When she was gone, Rabbitman sat up and rubbed his head. 'A chance to return to the Reverend Penny Farthing?' suggested Bobbi.

* * *

On Tottenham Court Road the Reverend Penny Farthing helped the verger to his feet and they crossed the road together, back towards All Saint's church. But, not long after starting out, they were stopped again, this time at the corner of Tottenham Street and Charlotte Street. There a voice called out, 'Halt! Who goes there?' A young man appeared, little more than a boy, holding an archaic looking rifle. 'Oh, it's you vicar,' said the young man. 'I thought you might be one of those Feds.'

'You shouldn't call them that, Spike,' said Penny. 'You know they don't like it.'

'It's just daft slang vicar,' replied Spike. 'Between the boys. We don't call it them to their faces.' Spike moved closer to the verger and mumbled, 'Beside which, they have real bullets in their guns.'

As he spoke, Spike noticed blood on the verger's forehead. 'Hey! What's happened to the verger?' he said loudly. 'He's bleeding.'

'One of those Feds,' answered Penny. 'But I think he'll be alright. It's just a graze really.'

'Yes, I'm alright vicar,' said the verger. 'It was the shock more than anything.'

'Which one of them was it?' asked Spike. 'There's some really nasty'uns you know.'

'I don't know,' said the verger. 'But he was nanti dish. A big omi with piggy ogles, a meese eek, broken pots and slimy black riha!'

'Speak English, verger,' said Penny. 'You're not in Piccadilly now.'

'Sorry vicar,' said the verger. 'I think the knock has left me scatty. Can I sit down?'

Spike took the verger's arm and helped him to sit on the cold concrete kerb at the side of the road. 'Captain Manning isn't going to like this,' said Spike.

'Don't tell him Spike!' said Penny, more sharply than she intended. 'I mean, we don't want to start another incident with the Rabbitman Guards.'

'No,' agreed Spike. 'But they've been bothering us a lot lately. This afternoon three of them were looking for you.'

'I knew it,' said the verger. 'That guardsman has reported us.'

'Don't be silly Mr Yates,' said Penny, seeming to forget her sympathy for the verger's injury. 'That just happened. Spike said they were looking for me this afternoon.'

'That's right,' said Spike. 'Jock and Mr Godley dealt with them, but they didn't say what they wanted.'

'Well it couldn't have been anything too serious,' said Penny. 'Or that foul man we just met would have taken us in.'

'Even so, vicar,' said the verger. 'I don't like it. I don't like it at all!'

'And then there was a woman looking for you,' said Spike.

'What woman?' asked Penny. 'What did she want?'

'I don't know,' replied Spike. 'Uncle Alfred – I mean Sargent Winston – spoke to her.'

Increasingly aware of the cold night air, Penny and the verger said their goodbyes to Spike and continued on their journey. They turned left at

Cleveland Street, and rejoined Goodge Street
where it turns into Mortimer Street, walking until
Wells Street, and found themselves finally back at
All Saint's church in Margaret Street. It wasn't a
long walk, but the events of that evening made it
feel so.

Back in the church the verger said he was
feeling better, although in need of a lie down, and
he disappeared leaving Penny alone in the vestry.
She slept there now, the verger cobbling together
an *ad hoc* bed and a few home comforts for the her,
while he slept somewhere in the attic space. So it
was Penny who heard the knock at the church door
later that evening. It wasn't a threatening or
particularly demonstrative knock. It was almost
apologetic. Of course Penny knew the rules. She
and the verger both knew the rules. The
Archbishop had insisted on them being followed to
the letter by all churches outside the enclaves. No
more church services after dark. No strangers to be
admitted to the church after dark. No calls at
church doors to be answered after dark. Penny

knew these were prudent precautions in these imprudent times, and she and the verger had always abided by them, even though contact with the Archbishop, now resident in the Canterbury Enclave, was very intermittent these days. Penny certainly had no reason to believe the rules had changed. And yet, that night, she opened the door. As she did so she was faced with a woman she recognised. It was the woman who had approached her in the street, near the PIO.

Without looking up, the woman said, 'I need to speak to you father.'

'Father?' queried Penny.

The woman looked up for the first time, realised the vicar was a woman, and apologised. 'I'm sorry,' she said. 'I mean mother.'

Penny laughed gently. 'We don't usually get called that. If you want to be formal, call me reverend, or vicar. But I prefer people to use my name. It's Penny.'

'Thank you, reverend,' said the woman, looking down again. Penny couldn't help feeling the woman didn't want to look into her eyes.

'Come in,' said Penny, breaking the Archbishop's rules even more. On this day, of all days, she thought, rules like that shouldn't apply. And somehow this woman seemed different. *Different to what?* The Reverend Penny could not have said.

The woman entered and walked as far as the main aisle of the church. There she turned and looked up at the high altar, and seemed about to bow before it. Whether it was the realisation she was in an Anglican church that stopped her, or some other unseen force, the woman only half-stooped, aborting the gesture almost the moment she started. Penny saw this, but said nothing. Had the Archbishop been there she might have told Penny to throw the Catholic out, but the Archbishop was so far away, and who could say whether her rules even applied to All Saint's Margaret Street any more? So why should Penny listen to a distant Archbishop? Why shouldn't she follow an older Christian rule, especially on that night, one that said we are all God's children, and that we are all brothers and sisters, and that we are all equal.

'What is your name dear,' Penny asked.

'Angela,' replied the woman. 'My name is Angela. Angela Witney.'

'You are welcome, Angela,' said Penny. 'Can I get you anything? Some tea perhaps.'

'No,' said Angela. 'I –'

The woman stopped, almost as though the effort of saying 'I' was too much. Was that it? thought Penny. The loss of 'I', the loss of self ?

'You look familiar,' said Penny. 'I mean, I know you tried to approach me in the street. But familiar from before that.'

'I –' said the woman again, but again she stopped.

'I think,' said Penny, 'you do need some tea. It's weak stuff. We have to reuse the tea bags and they're not the best anyway. No biscuits either, I'm afraid. But maybe we'll raid the Communion wafer tin and use a few of those. I am sure the Lord will not object to being dunked in a mug of Red Label for a good cause.'

The woman sniffed, almost letting out a laugh. 'Do you think I'm a good cause?' she asked.

'Anyone is a good cause who asks for help,' replied Penny. 'Although don't ever tell the Archbishop I said that. It's not Church policy any more.'

With these warm words the Reverend Penny Farthing led Angela into the vestry where she lit a camping gas stove, filled a kettle with water and placed it on the flame. She then began the process of finding a used tea bag that still looked as though it had some life left in it – what she jokingly called the Lazarus Blend – and put it in a small metal tea pot. Once there, with the kettle boiled, it was doused in boiling water.

'Sorry, no milk or sugar I'm afraid,' said Penny. 'But as promised,' she added with a flourish, 'the body of our Lord will serve as a biscuit.' She held up a metal tin, holding the lid open while Angela tentatively reached inside and pulled out a single Communion wafer. 'Take a few,' said Penny. 'They're rather thin.' Angela reached in again and took enough of the wafers to imitate an old-fashioned Rich Tea biscuit, at least if you stacked them one on top of the other.

'Thank you,' said Angela, sipping the tea. Her voice was stronger now, as though the impromptu Eucharist really had performed a minor miracle. 'You will probably think I'm mad,' said Angela after a while.

'Will I?' asked Penny. 'I doubt it. It's a mad mad world.'

'True,' agreed Angela. 'That's why –' Again she stopped.

'Have another biscuit,' suggested Penny.

Fortified, Angela continued. 'Reverend. Do you believe in the devil?'

'It's a strange question to ask a vicar,' replied Penny. 'It kind of goes with the territory.'

Angela smiled. 'Perhaps.'

'Yes, perhaps indeed,' agreed Penny. 'A few days ago I would have said evil exists,' continued Penny. 'Inside all of us I mean. But perhaps not the devil outside of us. But it's funny, this evening I saw an interview on television and –' Penny stopped short. 'You!' she said. 'It was you. On the news this evening. You presented the evidence.'

'Yes,' said Angela. 'I am the person who gave the world proof that the devil exists.'

'Good God!' said Penny slowly, forgetting herself and her location. *'You!'*

'But now I have to ask you something,' continued Angela. She seemed much stronger now, as though fortified by more than tea. She seemed to have an urgent determination to do what she had to do. 'Reverend, I want you to hear my confession.'

'Me?' asked Penny. 'Why me?'

'Because you're a priest. Or a vicar,' said Angela. 'Isn't that what you do? Hear the confessions of sinners. Doesn't that go with the territory too?'

'It's not really in the Anglican tradition,' said Penny. 'I mean, it's not forbidden, and I know some vicars do hear confessions. But it's not really something I do. Wouldn't you just like to pray on your own? Or maybe see a Catholic priest.'

Angela grabbed Penny's arm tightly, and for the first time Penny thought letting this woman into her church was a mistake. 'I need you to hear my confession,' Angela said again. 'Don't worry. You cannot forgive me. I cannot be forgiven. There is no absolution for my sin. But I must have my confession heard. And by you. It must be you.'

Penny was disturbed. *Why me?* she asked herself in her head.

'It has to be you,' said Angela, seeming to read Penny's thoughts. 'It has to be you, because something is going to happen. Soon. Tonight. I don't know what. Something. I don't even know if it will be good or bad, just something. And I need you to hear my confession before it does. There isn't time to find anyone else.'

Penny felt even more disturbed by Angela's claim something would happen. It sounded like a threat. Only when Angela uttered the word, please, with such desperation, did Penny relax. No, not relax. Relent. She relented as though the plea was not uttered by the woman in front of her, but from somewhere deep inside the darkness that surrounded them in that little room. It seemed like a divine darkness, almost alive and watching them, as if they were actors in a Caravaggio painting lit by candlelight. She felt almost compelled to agree.

'Alright,' said Penny. 'If you insist. I will.'

'Thank you,' said Angela quietly. 'Reverend, have you heard of the Catholic Workers' Guild?'

'Of course!' said Angela with genuine excitement in her voice. 'I used to have some dealings with them. A long time ago. It was all unofficial, of course. I never thought the Archbishop would approve. What with them being Catholics and anarchists. I don't know which she would have disliked more, the Catholicism or the anarchism, but it meant I had to keep it low key. But we worked on a few anti-racism projects together.'

'Then you will know,' interrupted Angela, 'we, members of the Guild I mean, left London some time ago?'

'Yes,' said Penny. 'You mean you were part of the CWG? Didn't you all move to Sussex to start a commune or something?'

'We moved to Ditchling,' said Angela. 'Life was getting so hard in London we thought we would take a group of the most vulnerable people and start living a simple life in the countryside.'

'I thought you were a Catholic when you came into the church,' said Penny. 'You gave it away when you passed the altar.'

'Nominally,' said Angela. 'I'm nominally Catholic. Lapsed I suppose. Not so long ago I would have said I am an atheist. Before I mean. Although not now. Either way, the Guild didn't insist on people being practising Catholics or even religious. As long as you were willing to work, as best you could for the community, you were welcome. Everyone was equal. We voted on everything, and the community flourished. We grew our own food, and baked our own bread, and for the first time since things started to go wrong in the country, I was happy. We were all happy. We even thought we would make our own wine.'

'Wine!' exclaimed Penny, remembering the verger's blunder with the castor oil. 'But how?'

'We took over some fields with grape vines in them,' said Angela. 'There are a lot of abandoned farms down there. We didn't know how to turn grapes into wine, but we started tending the plants, and we would have worked it out. That was my job you see. Looking after the grape vines. Last spring, I took on the job of tying the new shoots to the stakes that supported the vines. We had no machinery, so it was all done by hand. By me. I'm not sure there even is a machine that can do work like that. Anyway, I loved it, even in the spring rain, checking each vine for new growth and tying it to a stake. I felt like a character from a medieval illumination. All I needed was Noah or Job lying on a couch in front of me and it would have been an exact match. It felt like Paradise.'

'And then it went wrong?' prompted Penny.

'Once the vines were tied in, I had an idea we needed to make sure they were safe from pests,' said Angela, seeming to ignore the vicar's prompt, but in her own mind heeding it. 'I thought every caterpillar and beetle would head straight for the new grapes. But they didn't touch them. Father Nouwen called it a miracle.'

'Father Nouwen?' repeated Penny. 'Father Henri Nouwen? I know him. He is still with you?'

'Yes,' said Angela. 'We don't – didn't – have leaders, but Father Nouwen was considered –' Angela paused. 'A sensible voice. That's what you need in groups like that. Not leaders, but sensible voices. So we all look up to him even though he tells us not to. Anyway, the insects didn't touch the vines, or the slowly swelling grapes, all through the summer, until September, when the fruit started to ripen.'

'Then the insects started to eat the grapes?' asked Penny.

'Not the insects,' said Angela. 'Birds. Hundreds of them. Father Nouwen told me not to worry. He said there were plenty of grapes for us and the birds, and that a few scarecrows would cut our losses.'

'But they didn't?' asked Penny.

'Yes they did,' said Angela. 'Father Nouwen was right. He was always sensible you see.

Live with nature, he'd tell us. *Don't fight her.* But I was just angry at all these birds eating the grapes I had grown, even though there was plenty left for us to make wine. I couldn't say anything. Father Nouwen was always so reasonable. Let's share what we have, he'd keep saying. With each other and the birds. So I had to bottle it up inside. That's when I was at my weakest. It's when he struck.' Angela fell silent.

'Who struck?' asked Penny. 'Father Nouwen?' Angela just looked at Penny as though she had said the most ridiculous thing in the world.

'Father Nouwen? No of course not. Him!' Angela leaned forward as though fearful saying his name would conjure him forth. 'Lucifer,' she whispered.

Somewhere in the church a door or window banged loudly, and soon the verger appeared. 'Sorry vicar,' said the verger. 'I didn't realise you had company. One of the window latches has gone. I'll do a temporary fix now to keep us safe tonight and try and mend it properly in the morning.' Without waiting for a reply the verger was gone. Penny looked at Angela, and saw she was terrified.

'He's here,' said Angela quietly. 'He is in here.'

'Who?' asked Penny.

'Lucifer,' gasped Angela. 'I must finish my confession quickly. He saw me out in the fields one day. I was trying to get one of those stupid scarecrows to stand up, and he just strode along the row of vines and started helping me. At first he didn't say a word, he just helped. I thought he might be a new member of the Community, so I just let him, but then I noticed how he was dressed. It was how people used to dress, in the city I mean, in the old days. In a sharp suit, with an ironed shirt, a tie and beautiful turned out trousers. And polished shoes that might have just been bought in Jermyn Street, as it was two or three decades ago. I told him he shouldn't dress like that to work in the fields, but he said I needn't worry. He was very charming. Handsome too. But you would expect a devil to be charming. And handsome. Wouldn't you?'

Angela seemed to be waiting for an answer from Penny, so she said, 'Not always. I mean, if he exists.' Immediately Penny regretted what she said.

'You don't believe me,' said Angela. 'You think I'm imagining Lucifer visited me.'

'I didn't say that,' said Penny, although if she was honest she did doubt the existence of a devil who appeared in fields and helped put up scarecrows. Before that evening, before the proof she had seen on the BBC news, she would have said she doubted the existence of any devils. For her Christianity was a kind of community work, not a matter of belief in saints, or virgin births, or devils, or even God. That's why she had refused to join the Archbishop when she ran away to the safety of the Canterbury Enclave. She had stayed, with the verger, in central London, to help as best she could, the lost and destitute, and the ever-growing army of prostitutes, of all genders and ages, now plying their trade on the city's streets to earn a few euro or dollars to buy a little food to eat. It was a futile task, she knew that, but whether it made any difference had very little to do with God or the devil, Penny has always thought. 'Tell me your confession,' Penny continued. 'That's what matters.'

'Yes,' agreed Angela. 'That's what matters. Lucifer said he could rid me of the problem of the birds in an instant if I wanted him to. I just laughed, so he offered to prove it. He looked heavenward for one moment, and there was this strange rippling through the air, almost like a heat haze – *you know?* – and suddenly all the birds flew away. I asked him what he'd done and he just said he'd suggested to the birds they would have a better future sticking to the wild ground surrounding the Community. I remember he sounded almost menacing when he'd said he could be very persuasive, but I let it pass. But it was very true. Like Eve in Paradise, and the birds in those fields, I was ready to be persuaded.'

'Persuaded to do what?' asked Penny.

'To sell him my soul,' said Angela. 'You see that's what he wanted. To buy my soul. You could say getting rid of my bird problem was a kind of loss leader. He was just using it to prove he could do things. Do magic I mean. It was a way of persuading me to sell my soul for something bigger. Something much better.'

'Angela,' said Penny, gently but sternly. 'I know these things might seem real, but you know there is no such thing as magic. Maybe this man came and did some tricks. Maybe it was a coincidence that the birds flew away. They probably saw him dressed so strangely in the field and got spooked. Like you did. But that doesn't mean magic exists and it doesn't mean this man was the devil.'

'Lucifer,' said Angela with a surprising sense of insistence.

'I beg your pardon?' said Penny.

'Lucifer. His name was Lucifer. I got the impression, there isn't just one devil. Like *the Devil*, I mean. There are lots of them I think. So this one was called Lucifer. Maybe that also means there isn't one God. Maybe there is just a lot of angels and saints, or something equivalent to all the devils.'

'I leave those questions to theologists,' replied Penny evasively.

'Well, I can tell you,' said Angela, 'Lucifer is a devil. Perhaps not the devil, but a devil, and he came to me in that field, and he offered me a good price for something as insignificant, as he called it, as my soul.'

Before that evening Penny had been no more convinced of the existence of the human soul than she was of the devil, devils, God or gods. It made her feel guilty for a moment that she didn't believe in what a vicar is meant to believe in. 'And did you sell him your soul?' asked Penny, already suspecting the answer.

'Oh yes,' replied Angela. 'How could I refuse. The offer was too good to refuse.'

'The offer to rid the Community of pests?' asked Penny, thinking the offer too poor to accept.

Angela looked at Penny in confusion for a moment before laughing loudly. 'Pests!' she exclaimed. 'Yes, I suppose you could say he offered to rid us of our pests.'

'I don't understand,' said Penny. 'What did this devil offer you?'

'He told me he could give me anything,' said Penny. 'I could go and live in one of the enclaves, or in Freedonia, or Europe, as a very wealthy woman. But he knew I wouldn't take those offers. He led me very skilfully. He told me how he had taken the souls of Rabbitman, and Balloonhead, and Mr Floppy, and all those other creeps who had ruined the world with their lies, in return for them becoming great men, powerful men, rich men. He said he could make me President of Freedonia, or reform Englandshire with me as its queen, or create a whole new world, just for me. Anything. He could do anything he said. All I had to do was ask.'

'And you said yes,' said Penny quietly.

'I said yes,' echoed Angela.

'And what did you ask for?'

'I asked him to let me tell the truth and for it to be believed,' said Angela. 'I asked him to let me tell the truth about Rabbitman, and Balloonhead, and Mr Floppy, and all the others, that they had sold their souls to the devil, that they had bought power and corrupted the world, by selling their souls to the devil, and that the world would listen, and that the world would believe me because it is the truth.'

'And?' asked Penny.

'I told you,' said Angela, sounding irritated. 'I said yes. I said yes and Lucifer delivered on his promise. I was able to tell the world the truth. I saw you at the soup kitchen tonight. You saw me the on the television there, telling the truth. But —' Angela stopped.

'But?' Penny prompted.

'But the devil always cheats you, even when you get what you ask for.'

'How has he cheated you?' asked Penny.

'I told the truth, the truth was heard, and the truth was believed,' explained Angela. 'There is not a person alive anywhere in the world today who does not know that Rabbitman only got to be president by selling his soul to the devil. I got my wish by selling mine.' Penny looked straight at Angela, whose eyes were glistening with tears in the candlelight. 'What he didn't tell me,' Angela continued, 'is that no one would care. Your own Archbishop was on that programme with me, and all she could say is that we all know the rich and powerful cut corners to become rich and powerful, but it doesn't make them bad people. I tried to argue that selling your soul to the devil is not just cutting corners, but she said the Church needs to move on from old-fashioned ideas about good and evil. I pointed out all the lies that were told, and are still being told, but she didn't care. Nobody cares, everyone believes me, like some inverse Cassandra, but no one cares. The truth does not win over the lies. I sold my soul and got nothing.'

Penny sat in silence. She had watched the BBC news interview with Angela, and she had heard about Rabbitman selling his soul to the devil. Balloonhead too. And Mr Floppy, and all the others. And she had thought *so what? It doesn't surprise me. That lot always do. Who cares?* It was just as Angela described. No one cared. Not even someone like Penny.

A strange sensation filled Penny's stomach, and she almost had an unstoppable urge to fly from the room and vomit, as though some poison flowing through her body was being purged, some inner corruption of which she had been unaware for so long. She realised telling the truth was not enough. The corruption of the lies needed purging.

As this truth dawned on Penny, a profound darkness seemed to settle on the little vestry, extinguishing the last of the candles as it burned the last of its wax. *Eli, Eli, lama sabachthani?* the darkness seemed to be saying. Except Penny knew it was not the darkness speaking, but a voice in the dark, mocking and diabolical.

A loud knock at the door broke this bleak reverie. It burst open, terrifying the two women inside, as though they each expected the devil himself to enter. Instead it was Captain Manning.

'Vicar, I must speak to you at once!' he shouted.

§6

Very soon after calling her daughter downstairs to help with the chores, Angela's mother decided having the assistance of a bad-tempered eight-year-old was worse than having no help at all. And, like most children her age, Angela was wise to this lesson. The phrases, *leave it, I'll do it* and *watch what you're doing,* punctuated the air, and it was not long before Angela's mother had sent her little angel back upstairs, with a relatively mild rebuke that perhaps she was being *a selfish little madam.*

Once returned to her balcony on the landing, Angela picked up Rabbitman, stroked his head and gave him a little kiss by way of an apology for having tossed him aside so unceremoniously. Rabbitman was pleased, and suggested they get on with the play.

'Yes,' agreed Angela. 'But I've forgotten where we were.'

'Rabbitman was about to ask Bunny to sacrifice her soul to save him,' said Bobbi. 'At least I think that's what was about to happen. Titivillus is trying to persuade him to.'

* * *

Having inexplicably lost the services that night of six butch men from the Sixty-Sixth Detachment, Bunny had decided to go to bed early and alone. The sting of the chlorhexidine she had rinsed around her mouth for a full ten minutes before retiring was still being felt, making her tongue and gums burn. It wasn't surprising. She had used up half a bottle trying to rid herself of the taste of Rabbitman's taco-scented semen. So when she heard Rabbitman back in her room her heart sank as she thought of having to go through the whole process once again before getting any sleep that night.

For Rabbitman the journey to Bunny's bedroom was just as disturbing. One moment he was looking at Titivillus, standing in the Rabbitman Room, in front of the blazing fire, the next he was looking at Bunny, lying in her bed, illuminated only by the soft glow of the child's nightlight she still insisted be set next to her bed.

'I didn't hear you come in,' said Bunny stretching her arms and sitting up.

'Bunny, sweetheart,' said Rabbitman, sitting on the bed next to her. 'You know I love you don't you?'

'Of course Daddy,' said Bunny. 'And I love you.'

'I know that, sweetheart,' said Rabbitman. 'So if I asked you to do something for me – I mean something to show that you love me – you would wouldn't you?'

Bunny put her young arms around the old man's large waist and rested her head against his body. Rabbitman in turn put one of his fat old arms around her. 'If you mean will I put my tongue in your ass again,' said Bunny, 'you know I will do it if you want me to. I didn't really mind doing it, it's just –'

Rabbitman coughed in a rare moment of embarrassment, stopping Bunny from finishing her sentence. He was aware Titivillus was probably listening to their conversation. 'No, it's not that,' he said.

'Well if you want to stick your weenie in my ass, you know I don't mind that,' said Bunny. 'You don't usually ask.'

Rabbitman coughed again. 'No, no, it's not that,' he said uncoupling his arm from her body. 'I mean, if I needed something from you. Something really, really important. Maybe something that would save my life. You would say yes wouldn't you?'

'You mean like giving you one of my kidneys or my lungs or something?'

'Yes, like one of your kidneys,' said Rabbitman eagerly. 'Let's say I needed one of your kidneys. If my life depended on it, you would agree wouldn't you?'

Bunny looked thoughtful for a moment. For her thoughts were an unwelcome disturbance. They flickered over her smooth face like cumulous clouds flitting over an otherwise perfect cyan sky. 'You know I do love you Daddy,' she said like a naughty child about to admit to being very, very

118

naughty. Rabbitman recognised the tone of voice, and the coquettish tilt of Bunny's head that went with it. He knew it from the countless sex games they played together. 'I have been a very, very naughty girl, Daddy,' Bunny would say. 'And I need to be punished.' But this time Rabbitman was dreading the next sentence to come from Bunny's pretty little mouth, on her pretty little face, on her pretty little body, on all of which he had spent so much money making so pretty. 'But I couldn't risk having a scar. You wouldn't want me to have a scar would you, Daddy? Besides, couldn't we pay someone to give you their kidney or lungs? Or you could order someone to do it. Or maybe just take them from some prisoner in jail.'

Rabbitman was disappointed. But he rallied on the hope that Bunny might say yes if she knew there wouldn't be a scar. 'What if it wasn't my kidney or my lungs sweetheart?' he asked. 'What if it was something you couldn't see, and which wouldn't leave a scar?'

'Like what, Daddy?' asked Bunny.

'Well, let's say I asked you to give up your soul for me,' said Rabbitman. 'Would you do that?'

Bunny gave a short girlish giggle. 'You mean like that film Ghost Rider?' she asked. 'I don't think so,' she added quickly in almost a petulant tone.

'You don't think so?' echoed Rabbitman, a hint of anger now entering his voice.

Bunny managed what came close to a thoughtful expression on the limited range of emotions that could express themselves on her face. 'No. I don't think so. I don't, like, believe in God and all that. But I do believe in, like, something. You know, like ghosts and UFOs and things. So I wouldn't want to end up, like, punished by witches or something.'

Rabbitman stood up. Now he was angry. Very angry. It wasn't just that his wife and daughter were simultaneously denying something he thought should be given to him without a second thought, especially after all he had done for her. It was that he found, possibly for the first time in his life, the sound of a grown woman talking like a child grating. Up to now he had always liked women who did that, sought them out even, but now he was talking about his life, and his soul, and he wanted an adult to talk to. An adult to reason with. But with Bunny it was like trying to reason with an eight-year-old on why she should give up her jelly and ice cream. 'Listen, sweetheart,' Rabbitman said as calmly as he could manage. 'I need you to do this for me. I am your daddy.'

'I know, Daddy,' replied Bunny. 'But I really couldn't. I don't want to. I don't want to.' Bunny was getting more petulant the more Rabbitman asked. Still, too much depended on Bunny agreeing, so Rabbitman persisted. But still the answer was the same. 'No, Daddy. No. No. No,' she said.

Quite what Rabbitman did next he couldn't really remember. He would have denied, and believed his own denial, that he had lunged at Bunny, and that she began screaming. He would have denied, and believed his denial, that he had picked her up by the lapels of her bunnykins pyjamas, his fist grabbing as much flesh from her expensively remodelled breasts as it did pyjama fabric. He would have denied, and believed his denial, that he swore at her and accused her of being an ungrateful whore. He would have denied, and believed his denial, that at some point he hurled her body, as easily as some child's soft toy, across the room, so she hit the wall hard, and landed heavily on the floor. He would have denied, and believed his own denials in all of these things, or have said she did them herself. But he did do it.

All of it.

Believe me.

It's the truth.

§7

It was getting dark. Angela knew it was time to stop
playing on the landing, and to move downstairs to
the safety of the light in the main living room.
Angela was afraid of the dark, and aside from
manifesting itself in her continuing insistence on
sleeping in her parents' bedroom, this meant she
refused to venture onto the landing alone after
dark, where the light bulb had blown years earlier
and had, for an inexplicable reason, never been
replaced.

'Does that mean we'll never hear the end
of the story?' asked Nou Nou.

'We'll carry on tomorrow,' said Angela,
standing and eager to get away before the shadows
grew too dark and threatening.

'You'll forget,' said Nou Nou. 'You always
forget.'

'No I don't!' protested Angela.

'Yes you do,' mumbled the toys in unison.

'Well,' said Angela, surprised at the general criticism directed against her. 'Bobbi will remind me and we'll carry on.'

'But that only works if you remember to ask Bobbi tomorrow,' said Nou Nou. 'You'll forget to do that.'

'I won't!' insisted Angela, becoming increasingly disturbed at the darkness enveloping her. 'I won't!' she said again, running to the stairs, and down them as though the darkness itself was chasing her. 'I won't!'

'You won't what?' asked Angela's mother as Angela almost crashed into her at the bottom of the stairs.

'I won't forget,' said Angela sweetly, smiling with relief at being met by her mother.

'She will,' said Rabbitman to the other toys upstairs.

'For once I agree with you,' said Bobbi. 'But at least we can continue with *our* story.

* * *

124

'Captain Manning!' said Penny as the Captain, followed by his second in command, Sargent Winston, Spike and the verger all burst in the room. 'This is really unacceptable. This is not just the vestry any more you know. It's my living quarters.'

'I know that vicar,' said Manning. 'My apologies, but I have to speak to you on a matter of urgent business.'

'I tried to stop him, vicar,' said the verger, poking his head around Manning's portly body. 'I tried to stop him, but he wouldn't take no for an answer.'

'Alright, Mr Yates,' said Penny. 'What is it Captain Manning, you can see I am with a parishioner.'

'I thought we'd agreed,' continued Manning, 'you would give me prior-warning of any large meetings at the church.'

'I hardy think one parishioner constitutes a large meeting, Captain Manning,' said Penny.

'I am not talking about you and the young lady here,' said Manning. 'I mean the large crowd assembled outside. Now I don't want to be forced to fire warning shots over their heads to disperse them.'

'We can't shoot warning shots can we Uncle Alfred? We don't have any bullets,' said Spike *sotto voce*.

'Quiet boy!' called Manning.

'I was just saying, Uncle Alfred,' said Spike before going into a sulk.

'Now if this is a gathering you have organised,' continued Manning, 'I do think I should have been told. We live in difficult times and we don't want to provoke our neighbours, the Rabbitman Guards. They can be get very worked up about this kind of thing.'

'I can assure you, Captain Manning,' said the vicar, 'I don't know anything about a crowd. Mr Yates, do you know what Captain Manning is talking about?'

The verger pushed himself forward again. 'I don't know who they are,' he said. 'But Captain Manning is right. There is a big crowd outside. And they seem to want you, vicar.'

'Perhaps it's like the French Revolution, Uncle Alfred,' said Spike. 'And they want to haul the vicar off to the guillotine.'

'Be quiet boy!' shouted Manning. 'Can't you see you're upsetting the vicar?'

'I was just saying, Uncle Alfred,' said Spike, returning to his sulk. As for the vicar, she seemed perfectly composed.

'He might be right,' agreed the verger. 'We should get the vicar to safety. They do look like an ugly mob.'

'Agreed,' said Manning. 'My men will create a diversion at the front, and the vicar, the verger and this young woman will make a run for it out the back. Winston, you go to the front with Private Spike and start the diversion.'

Winston looked nonplussed. 'What sort of diversion would you suggest, sir?' he asked.

'I don't know,' said Manning testily. 'Use your initiative.'

'Don't do anything of the kind,' said Penny standing up. 'This is my church and I will say what happens here. And whatever happens I am not running away. Besides which, your plan has one serious flaw.'

'Which is?' asked Manning.

'The church doesn't have a back door,' said Penny. 'What I suggest we do instead is go outside, and talk to the crowd to see what they want.'

'But I don't like it vicar,' said the verger. 'I don't like it. They don't seem very Christian.'

'Does anyone these days, Mr Yates?' said Penny, standing. 'Does anyone!'

Penny, the verger and the brave men of the local militia left the vestry and walked through the dark church to the oak door which stood firm, barred against the noisy mob outside. Only Angela remained behind, alone in the little vestry, in which the gloom had been alleviated, a little, by the light from a single candle the verger had brought with him and left behind. But, despite the candle's best efforts, the corners of the room seemed stubbornly stuck in deep shadow. And it was from one of those corners, from the darkest shadow in the room, that a familiar voice could be heard. 'Don't be frightened Angela,' it said. But Angela was frightened. It was the voice of Lucifer.

'You!' Angela tried to cry out, but the word was more croaked than spoken.

'Don't be frightened,' the voice said again, this time with the body Lucifer attached to it as he stepped forward into the candlelight.

'Who should I fear if not you?' asked Angela with bitterness. 'You tricked me.'

'Did I?' asked Lucifer. 'You asked me to give you the power to reveal the truth about Rabbitman. And the others. Did I fall short?'

'No, but you knew people wouldn't care,' cried Angela. 'You knew and you said nothing.'

'Things like that are not certain,' said Lucifer, almost defensively. 'How could I know?'

'You knew,' said Angela. 'You always know. Your contracts are never gambles. Not for you anyway. You always collect on your debt.'

'Do I?' asked Lucifer. 'You seem to know a lot about me. But I think more from the movies than reality. Lucifer looked out of the open door of the vestry into the church. For most people, the darkness of the nave would have been impenetrable, but Lucifer saw through the darkness to the far end of the building where the vicar, the verger, Captain Manning and his men were debating what the large crowd outside might want.

'I like your vicar,' Lucifer said. 'I'd like to do something for her.'

'Leave her alone,' cried Angela. 'Can't you see she's a good person.'

Lucifer smiled. 'That's why I want to do something for her,' he said.

'Dear God!' cried Angela. 'Please no! Not her.'

'And I like the verger too,' continued Lucifer, ignoring Angela's plea. 'Especially when he smiles. Not so often now, I know, but sometimes he still does. When he thinks about Earl's Court.'

'I don't understand,' said Angela.

'Few people do,' said Lucifer. 'A friend of mine was speaking to a man not so long ago who claimed he was unique because he did understand. He thought it made him very smart, and that being so smart, at least in his own eyes, he was better than everyone else.'

'And what happened to him?' asked Angela.

'He threw himself into a furnace,' said Lucifer casually. 'Metaphorically speaking.'

'I think you throw everyone into the furnace,' said Angela bitterly. 'No, you trick people into opening the furnace door and throwing themselves in. I bet that's what happened to that poor man. You tricked him.'

'I'd save any tears you might have for him,' said Lucifer. 'He didn't just open the furnace. He built it, brick by brick. But this is grim talk. Why do you think I'm here Angela?'

'To take me to hell,' cried Angela weeping. 'I sold my soul for nothing. And now I must pay the price. All for nothing.'

Lucifer laughed. 'If you don't mind me saying, you are too certain of yourself, dear Angela. You think too much in black and white. You think *this is good,* and *this is a good person,* and *this is a good act.* And then you think *this is bad,* and *this is a bad person,* and *this is a bad act.'*

'It's called naivety,' replied Angela. 'Or stupidity. Yes, that's it, I was stupid. I poured a drop of pure water into a cesspit and was surprised it was still a cesspit.'

'And you think I should have warned you against that?' exclaimed Lucifer. 'Wasn't it obvious?'

'Yes, obvious,' said Angela, no longer weeping. Bitterness made her voice cold and hard. 'Like I said, stupidity. I didn't realise it was a cesspit. I didn't understand. Humanity is a cesspit, more impressed by the bling and bravado of a lying monster like Rabbitman, than the truth, no matter how extraordinary the truth.'

'You are too hard on yourself, dear Angela,' said Lucifer. 'Seeing things in black and white again. You knew all of this before you ever met me. The world was like this long before Rabbitman came on the scene. But you still told the truth. You still chose to tell the truth.'

'And now I will go to hell for it!' exclaimed Angela.

Lucifer laughed again. 'Tell me Angela, what do you think heaven and hell are?'

'Now whose being obvious?' said Angela.

'Your idea of things being obvious has proven unreliable so far,' said Lucifer with a touch of sarcasm in his voice. 'Why do you trust yourself on what heaven and hell must be like now? You were wrong before. Maybe you're wrong now.'

Angela felt like throwing the nearby candle at the handsome monster in front of her for his callousness. Instead she threw the challenge, 'Okay, enlighten me.'

'If you'll listen,' said Lucifer. 'It's a problem with you humans, you are so unable to listen to the truth when it's offered to you. Even you, dear Angela.' Angela stayed silent, half expecting to be told her fate in the fires of hell. So Lucifer continued. 'Tell me, do you like olives?'

'Olives?' replied Angela, struck by the incongruity of the question.

'Yes, olives,' said Lucifer. 'There's some on the table in front of you. Have some if you want.' Angela looked down, and as Lucifer had said a bowl of black Kalamata olives had appeared on the little table, next to the candle. But Angela was too wary of the devil to risk eating his food. She was not going to fall into the trap of Persephone. 'Do you like them?' repeated Lucifer.

'Yes,' said Angela, softly. 'When we used to have them. Years ago.'

'But you accept that not everyone likes olives?' asked Lucifer. 'That some people find them bitter and will spit them out?'

'Of course,' agreed Angela.

'And Coca-Cola?' asked Lucifer. 'Do you like Coca-Cola?' As he spoke, Lucifer pointed again to the little table where an old-fashioned glass bottle of cola had miraculously appeared.

'Coke,' said Angela distractedly, almost disbelieving the questions on her food preferences from a creature about to whisk her off to hell. 'I haven't seen it in –' Angela pulled herself together, coughed, and regained a sense of certainty in her voice. 'But no,' she said. 'I never really liked it. It was too sweet. For me.'

'But you'll agree,' said Lucifer, 'some people love the stuff. Not just children. Some adults too.'

'Yes, of course,' said Angela, 'but what has this –'

'But the olives are the same whether you find them too bitter or just right,' interrupted Lucifer. 'Isn't that so? And the Coca-Cola doesn't change if you find it too sweet or the taste of perfection? They are still the same olives and the same soft drink, so it must be the person that's different.'

'Why are you talking about these things?' asked Angela.

'Because, dear Angela,' said Lucifer, 'what if heaven and hell are like that?'

'I don't understand,' said Angela.

'What if heaven and hell are the same thing?' said Lucifer. 'What if angels and demons are the same beings, and even God and Satan are one and the same? What if it's just that some people see them as too bitter, and other people as too sweet, and some people find them just right?'

This time it was Angela's turn to laugh. 'You're trying to tell me that heaven and hell is an eternity of being forced to eat olives and drink Coke, and it just depends on whether you like them or not?'

'Not quite,' said Lucifer. 'That was an analogy. An attempt to explain that heaven and hell are what we each create as individuals, not places we are sentenced to. There is no heaven up there or hell down there, at least not in the way you think there is. There are just the worlds we forge for ourselves by our actions. What is it Marley says to Scrooge, "I wear the chain I forged in life. I made it link by link, and yard by yard; I girded it on of my own free will, and of my own free will I wore it." So what kind of hell do you imagine you have made for yourself, dear, dear Angela? You had no soul to sell, not to me or to anyone else. You just had choices, the choice of doing good or doing evil, and you chose to do good. "Blessed are they which do hunger and thirst after righteousness: for they shall be filled."'

Angela looked at Lucifer, and was aware that the sense of threat, or menace, that he seemed to exude only moments earlier was gone. Despite this, the depths of her fears meant it was difficult to accept what he was saying. 'How can there be no heaven or hell?' she asked. 'You're a devil?'

'Are you sure I'm not an angel?' asked Lucifer. Angela looked at Lucifer more intently than ever before. She realised she had never really looked at him properly, or if she had, she must have missed something about him. For the first time, he did seem more angelic than demonic. He hadn't sprouted wings and donned a white surplice, but then he had never had horns sprouting from his head or, to the best of her knowledge, cloven feet. In truth he looked the same, but he seemed different.

'You mean you're not here to take me to hell?' asked Angela.

'Of course not,' said Lucifer. 'That was never likely. That's why I was sent to you. When we give most people a free wish, they prove to be selfish. They will choose to do something for themselves, or something really bad. But we never thought that of you. It was a gamble, of course, but you, so to speak, backed the right horse. You're not going to hell. In fact you still have a long and happy life ahead of you. Not happy all the time, of course, but more happy than sad from now on.'

'And the contract?' said Angela.

'It's a myth,' said Lucifer. 'Like I said, you have no soul to sell. No one does.'

With tears of joy now filling her eyes, Angela suddenly leapt from her seat, put her arms around Lucifer's neck and kissed him. Despite all he had said, she still thought there was the slight whiff of sulphur in the air around him, but she put that down to her imagination. Yet, almost as soon as she had jumped up from her seat she pulled back.

'What's wrong?' he asked.

'But doesn't that mean, Rabbitman, and Balloonhead, and Mr Floppy, and all the rest of them will get off free? That there is no punishment waiting for them either?'

'Why do you think that?' asked Lucifer. 'I told you, we make our heaven or our hell in life, by the way we live our lives. I remember explaining the point to Dickens myself just before he wrote A Christmas Carol. We forge our own chains or we forge our own freedom. Rabbitman and Balloonhead have made terrible hells for themselves, trust me. There is no hope for them. It is not bitter olives Rabbitman will eat for all eternity. He has seen to that himself. Mr Floppy is different. He also has a very long life ahead of him, but he is being treated for his mental illness here on earth. At St George's Hospital in Tooting in fact. That's his hell. He's quite mad you know?'

'And the rest of us?' asked Angela. 'Who don't even care about the truth, are we mad too?'

'Of course you're all mad,' said Lucifer. 'But it's a difficult question, who is madder, the mad-man or the man who takes the mad-man seriously. Shall we go and find the vicar and the verger? They've been gone a very long time.'

The vicar, verger, Manning and Manning's men were still standing by the great oak door, debating what to do. 'I'm not sure they really sound angry,' said Penny. 'They sound almost desperate. So shall we see what they want?'

'I don't think that's a good idea, vicar,' said the verger. 'I'm not too keen on going the way of the saints.'

'I agree vicar,' said Manning. 'What do you think Winston?'

'Perhaps,' said Winston, 'it might be a good idea if you went out there first, Captain Manning. You might calm them down. With your gravitas.'

'Good idea,' agreed Manning. 'I can ask them what they want.'

'And that way if anyone shoots they'll hit you first,' added Winston.

'Ah,' said Manning. 'On second thoughts, perhaps we should barricade the door until they get bored and go away.'

'Oh for God's sake!' said Penny, pushing Manning aside and unbolting the door. Pulling the last of three wrought iron bolts aside, the door opened and Penny stepped outside.

Whether it was to give the vicar space to stand, or a sense of respect for her office, as soon as the door opened the crowd instinctively drew back. Penny stepped into the small courtyard garden that separated the church from Margaret Street, and looked at the crowd in front of her. It was vast, filling not only the courtyard, but much of Margaret Street beyond, at least from what she could see. When it was clear no shots were about to be fired, the verger, Manning and Manning's men followed Penny outside and stood, as amazed as she, at the sight of the crowd. Clearing her throat, Penny said loudly. 'Why are you here? What is it you want from me?'

At first there was no response from the crowd, but at last someone called out. 'We want to repent, vicar. We want God to forgive us.'

'Forgive you?' asked the vicar, unsure if she was addressing only the unknown voice from the crowd, or the whole crowd itself. 'You mean, all of you want forgiveness? For what?'

'We want God to forgive us. We have been so stupid,' cried another voice from the crowd. This time the plea for forgiveness was taken up by others, all crying out, 'We have been so stupid. Forgive us! Forgive us!'

Penny looked at the verger and Manning, but saw on their faces as much confusion as she knew must have been visible on her own. At that moment a man pushed his way through the crowd, and handed Penny a note. 'A message from the Archbishop,' he said. 'It's happening all over the country. Crowds outside churches, and mosques, and temples, and synagogues, all asking for God to forgive them. There's even a crowd outside the old headquarters of the British Humanist Society.'

'But forgiven for what?' asked Penny.

'They're asking to be forgiven their stupidity,' answered the messenger. 'As you will see from the Archbishop's note. But your orders are not to forgive anyone until an official policy has been formed. The synod is meeting now and consulting with the Freedonians. Until we have an official policy you just have to keep the crowd occupied.' With that, the messenger left, while Penny looked at her companions, all still bemused at what they could see, and what the Archbishop had ordered Penny not to do.

Penny looked at the crowd again, which was still asking her for God's forgiveness. 'This is ridiculous,' she said. 'How am I supposed to keep them occupied? We still don't know what they are asking forgiveness for.'

'They said it's for being so stupid, vicar,' said the verger.

'I know that Mr Yates, but how can I forgive them that?' asked Penny. 'It's not a sin. The Ten Commandments does not say *Thou Shalt Not be Stupid*. And what makes them think they have been stupid anyway?'

'Perhaps, you should ask them, vicar,' suggested Winston.

Penny nodded and called out: 'Tell me, why do you think you have been stupid? Why do you want forgiveness?'

'We listened to the devil,' cried a voice from the crowd. 'We followed the swivel-eyed loons! We followed Balloonhead!' shouted another.

'We voted for Fuxit!' cried another. At that moment three Freedonians, all Rabbitman Guards, pushed forward.

'Oh, look,' said Spike. 'It's those three Feds who were looking for you earlier, vicar.' The more dominant of the three Freedonians spoke up and cried out, 'We voted for Rabbitman! Can God ever forgive us?'

'This is ridiculous,' said Penny.

'I agree,' said Manning. 'One expects this kind of behaviour from Freedonians, but this is still Englandshire. All this wailing and gnashing of teeth. It's just not English. Winston tell these people to pull themselves together.'

'It is rather extravagant,' agreed Sargent Winston, ignoring Captain Manning's order. 'But perhaps you should say something to them Captain Manning. To calm them down. It will sound better coming from a superior officer.'

'Agreed!' said Manning, stepping forward without waiting to hear any objections from the vicar or verger. 'Now look here,' he began telling the crowd. 'We can see you're upset. But you really do have to pull yourselves together. You are all making fools of yourselves. All this – what did you call it Winston?'

'Extravagance, sir,' said Winston.

'That's right,' continued Manning. 'All this extravagance. It's unnecessary and melodramatic. That's what it is.'

'Oh dear,' said Spike. 'You seem to have upset them even more, Captain Manning. They seem to be getting awfully agitated.'

'Oh, stand aside Captain Manning,' said Penny. 'It's me they came to see not you. This is a Church matter.'

'I really think you should do something, vicar,' said the verger. 'It wouldn't take much for them to turn into a nasty mob.'

'You're right, verger,' agreed Penny. 'But what can I do?'

At that moment Angela and Lucifer appeared at the church door. 'Perhaps you should forgive them,' said Lucifer.

'Who are you?' asked Penny.

'Don't you recognise me?' asked Lucifer.

'Archbishop!' cried Penny. 'I'm so sorry, Archbishop. No, I didn't recognise you! It has been a long time.' Angela looked on in astonishment, unsure why Penny thought Lucifer was the Archbishop. 'I mean I had no idea you were visiting.'

'This situation calls for firm action,' said Lucifer as the Archbishop. 'I thought it required firm action from the top. No offence Lord, the top of the Church that is.'

'But what can we do?' asked Penny.

'First,' said Lucifer as the Archbishop, 'could you ask your verger to get up off his knees. I'm the Archbishop of Canterbury not the Pope.' Penny grabbed the verger's arm and pulled him to his feet. 'Now, Mr Yates,' said Lucifer, 'would you mind fetching that case of castor oil I believe you obtained this afternoon?' The verger disappeared for a few moments, returning with the castor oil. 'And now, if you would allow me to speak to your congregation, Reverend Farthing.' Penny stepped aside, leaving Lucifer to address the crowd. Lucifer, for his part, appeared to the assembled mass to be the very image of the Archbishop of Canterbury. And in that role he raised his hands and called out, 'People of London, what is it you want of the good Reverend Penny, and her honest verger, Mr Yates. What do you want them to do?' After a moment's silence a single cry went up from the crowd.

'We want to repent! Archbishop! Please ask God to forgive us? We beg you!'

'Repent you say,' shouted Lucifer, sounding increasingly like an old time Freedonian preacher. 'Repent! But you are sinners! All sinners! And sinners must go to hell!'

'No! No!' shouted the crowd. 'Forgive us our sins!'

'Forgive you?' asked Lucifer. 'But your sins are Legion. Who could forgive so many sins?'

'We beg you Archbishop,' cried the crowd. 'Forgive us our sins!'

'You ask God to forgive you, but you betrayed the one commandment he gave you that can never be forgiven,' shouted Lucifer, his finger jabbing towards the crowd, as though accusing one body. 'He told you to love your neighbour as you would be loved yourself. Who amongst you can claim to have followed that one simple command?'

'We know, we are sinners,' wailed the crowd.

'Yes you are sinners,' continued Lucifer. 'Mighty sinners. The devil stole into the garden of Englandshire one night and you listened to him. He came in the guise of a man, making easy promises to solve difficult things and you listened to him. He was a serpent who coiled his scaly tail around your hearts. Because you listened to him, you are sinners. You must go to hell!'

'No, no!' cried the crowd. 'Save us from our sins! Save us!'

'I cannot save you, sinners,' spat Lucifer. 'You listened to the devil in disguise. Who amongst you stood back and said "This creature lies"? Who amongst you said, "This monster will corrupt us"? Which of you said to your fellow men and women, "Stop up your ears against this monster and cast him out"? Not one. Not one of you! You all listened, and having listened you ate of the forbidden fruit of the Tree of Hatred, and clothed yourselves in the weeds of enmity, resentment and the sin of animus. No, I cannot save you. You are guilty of the greatest sin of all, the sin of stupidity! You must all go to hell.'

'No! No!' came the cry again from the crowd, as tears flowed amongst it. 'We were misled. Lead us to the right way!

'The right way! The right way you say!' cried Lucifer. 'Have you not learned from this sin. You ask for forgiveness, but you would still ask another to tell you right from wrong? Are you still stupid? Can not one of you not tell the good act from the bad for yourself? After all that has happened, have you no sense of morality? If you are truly sorry –'

'We are! We are!'

'– if you would truly repent your sin.'

'But we do! We do!' cried the crowd.

'Then listen again to the devil who beguiled you with charming words, spoken in the language of bonhomie over a pint of ale in a traditional English pub. Listen again to the ogre who dazzled you with his house of gold. Hear again the demons who taught you the language of contempt. Listen to them all again, but now judge them. Judge them not as I tell you they should be judged: judge them as they deserve to be judged!'

'We will! We will,' cried the people, a little hope now rising in their breasts. 'We will judge them and cast them out!'

'O no, you will not,' called out Lucifer, sounding almost like a pantomime comic.

'O yes, we will! We will! cried the people in unison. 'We will!'

'Do you really expect the Lord to believe you?' said Lucifer. 'The Lord who created the heavens and the earth, and all the creatures of the land, and the creatures of the air, and the creatures of the sea: the Lord who called out into the darkness, *Let there be light!* and there was light: the Lord who made all things. You expect Him to believe your easy promises? You expect the God of Love, who died to teach you how to live: you expect the unknowable God who lives beyond time and space – who gave you the simple commandment to love your neighbour – you expect Him to believe a word you say? Why should the Lord believe such a wayward flock?'

'Believe us!' called out the people. 'Forgive us Lord!'

'Do you truly repent your sins and reject the evil words of Rabbitman, and Balloonhead, and Mr Floppy, and all the other swivel-eyed loons?' asked Lucifer.

'We do! We do!' cried the people.

'And do you swear to follow the path of intelligence and enlightenment, loving your neighbours as you would each be loved yourselves, living in a spirit of harmony and friendship forever more?'

'We do! We do!' cried the people again.

'And do you forsake the populist rabble-rousers, who mould you into a braying mob, and lead you as a mob, straight into the open mouth of hell by scapegoating the weak, and demonising the powerless and poor?'

'We do! We do!' cried the people again.

'Then swear this to each other, and forgive each other, and believe in each other, if you dare to accept the word of your fellow men and women. If you truly repent, if you would be forgiven the sins of hatred and stupidity, turn not to God for forgiveness, but to those you have hurt. Turn to each other and embrace, and ask for forgiveness, and if you can find it in your own hearts to forgive, you are forgiven.'

'I do! I do!' cried every man, woman and child in front of the church. As they did so, they embraced and said to whoever stood next to them, *Forgive me brother* and *Forgive me sister,* and they were forgiven.

'Praise be!' cried out Lucifer with one final flourish 'And to mark this special night, and remind each of us of our promise to each other; and to recall the bitterness of the evil times into which we have been led, let each of us take a dose of castor oil on this night, and on the anniversary of this night, Christmas Eve, forever more. Purge the lies, and the sin of stupidity, from your bodies, as you would purge a worm from your guts. Purge your stomachs, to purge your souls.'

'Yes, give me castor oil!' called out every person in the crowd. 'I beg you, give me castor oil!'

As soon as this cry went up the verger's bottles of castor oil were passed around the crowd. Although most people took only a small sip of the foul syrup, some of the liberal zealots showed the depth of their repentance by downing whole bottles. Those with weaker stomachs quickly found themselves rushing away in search of a privy, or at least a privy-bush to relieve themselves behind. But, whether they took a teaspoon of castor oil, or a whole bottle, by the end of that night every man, woman and child in that crowd felt purged of their sins, and purged of the legacy of Rabbitman, and Balloonhead, and Mr Floppy, as readily as their bodies were purged of shit.

'I must leave you now,' said Lucifer to Penny. Without waiting for a goodbye in return, he walked briskly through the crowd, which seemed to divide before him like Moses parting the Red Sea, and in the minds of almost everyone present, the Archbishop was gone.

'She doesn't hang about,' said Manning. 'Does she Winston?'

'No, sir,' said Winston. 'But I suppose she is rather busy. There are *a lot* of people needing to repent.'

'Quite so,' said Manning. 'Which brings me to a rather delicate point vicar.' Manning coughed with embarrassment. 'I suppose I too should ask for forgiveness. You see, I was foolish enough to vote for some of those swivel-eyed loons. I mean I voted for Fuxit. Taken in by Balloonman as it were. It was all a long time ago, of course. But I was wrong. How about you Winston?'

'No,' said Winston calmly. 'I don't need to ask for forgiveness.'

'You don't?' asked Manning. 'Why not?'

'Well, you see,' continued Winston, 'I didn't vote for Balloonhead. Or to leave Europe.'

'You didn't?' said Manning.

'You needn't sound so surprised,' said Winston. 'Most people didn't.'

'But I thought it was fifty-two percent against Europe,' said Manning.

'Only if you exclude those who couldn't vote,' explained Winston. 'People under eighteen. And all the foreign nationals. Some of them had lived here for decades, paying taxes and national insurance, and working in state schools and the NHS, and things like that. But not one of them had a say over the future of the country. You could argue – *I mean you could argue* – it was as much their home as ours, and they should have had a say on its future, even if they didn't have a British passport.'

Manning coughed again. 'Yes, well when you put it like that.'

'Oh I do,' said Winston. 'And then when I looked at people like Balloonhead I just thought, what a nasty little man. He seemed to be all mouth and no chin you might say. I looked at him and I thought, I cannot bring myself to vote with you. Not with my background anyway?'

'What do you mean, your background?' asked Manning.

'My family were Huguenots,' explained Winston. 'Refugees from persecution who came to this country and found a home. They came a long time ago, of course, but they still came from somewhere else and asked for help, and they got help.'

'You told me your family came over with William the Conqueror,' said Manning.

'Yes, on my mother's side,' said Winston. 'But my father's family were Huguenots. The point is, I don't have to ask forgiveness. Not in the same way as you, anyway. My only sin, back then I mean, was not to stand up and say no, to Balloonhead and the swivel-eyed loons. I just kept quiet and let him get away with it. It was the easy option you see. People like him ruined the country because people like me didn't stand up and say *no*. We were the silent majority and we said nothing. Or, we didn't say anything loudly enough anyway.'

'Exactly,' said Manning, grateful for the small admission of guilt from his second in command. 'I don't think there's any point going over who was a leaver and who was a remainer. As you say, a long time ago. We all got into this mess together and now we'll have to get out of it together. So are we forgiven our sins, vicar? Winston and me?'

'You heard the Archbishop, Captain Manning,' said Penny. 'We're all forgiven as long as we forgive. *And we sin no more.* But there is one thing still bothering me, Captain Manning. The women in Goodge Street underground station. They are still there.'

'If I might interrupt with a suggestion,' said Winston.

'Yes, what is it?' said Manning sharply.

'If the women are in carriages in the tunnels,' continued Winston, 'why don't we use the tunnels from our end to rescue them? We could creep along the tunnels and bring the women back through them without the Freedonians even knowing. Not until it's too late at least. At the very least it would give us a head start, while they try to work out what is going on.'

'Brilliant,' said Manning. 'I was wondering when someone else would see that plan. Leave it to us, vicar, the women will be free by morning. We'll bring them to the church if we may. But you realise, Goodge Street is not the only Rabbitman underground club in the city?'

'I know, Captain Manning,' said Penny. 'But let's make a start at building a better world. Even if it's only one small step at a time.'

'Yes,' agreed Manning. 'One small step at a time. But I still think I would like some fire power to help us take that first step. Sargent Winston, do you see those three Freedonians? They have assault rifles on them. Go and see if they really are repentant, and if we can borrow them.'

'Uncle Alfred,' said Spike. 'I'd like an assault rifle. Can I have one please? Please Uncle Alfred.'

'Be quiet Frank,' said Winston. 'I really do think it would be better coming from you, Captain Manning. After all you do carry more authority. You are a captain after all.'

'Quite right,' said Manning. 'Come on. You too Spike. We have an operation to plan.'

§8

The next morning the toys sat on the landing balcony, waiting impatiently for Angela to come in from the snow and finish the performance. It was Sunday, and they knew the time between playing in the snow and going to church would be short. Given Angela's tendency to forget her plays from one day to the next, the toys feared they would never discover what happened to President Rabbitman if they had to wait until the afternoon to see Angela.

Luckily for them, Angela's mother called her daughter in early from playing outside, concerned the time it would take her to change from her cold wet clothes into something more suitable for church would make them late. Soon Angela appeared on the stairs, smiling at the toys. 'I have a new play,' she said, but was surprised to find the toys only groaned at the news.

'You promised you would not forget,' said Bobbi.

'Yes, you promised,' echoed Nou Nou.

'Forget what?' asked Angela.

'The story about Rabbitman,' said Nou Nou.

'What about Rabbitman?' said Angela, picking up the toy Rabbitman.

'The story about President Rabbitman,' said Rabbitman sternly. 'You remember?'

Angela looked puzzled. Usually her amnesia for the games she played was absolute from one day to the next, and affected the toys as much as herself. So why they should remember this game, when she did not, was a mystery. Perhaps Angela's childish mind, up to now filled with only the vague outline of memories – that she liked playing with her toys, that she preferred chocolate ice cream to vanilla, and that she was afraid of the dark – was slowly evolving into a more adult sense of reminiscence. But could the toys really pick up on that before Angela did?

'Oh, yes,' said Angela at last. 'I forgot. Sorry.'

* * *

In the Gold House, Rabbitman was surprised to find himself again in the Rabbitman Room, staring once again at Titivillus, still standing in front of the roaring fire. As the shock of what had happened in Bunny's bedroom cleared from his eyes, Rabbitman began to laugh. 'I get it. I get it. This is a Scrooge story,' he said. I'm Scrooge, I'm being shown my Christmas past, present and future. Okay, okay, I get it. I repent. I'll be a good boy from now on.' Titivillus looked at him in silence. 'So what's next?' asked Rabbitman. 'Don't tell me, I know. We're gonna visit little Balloonhead and you're gonna show me how we used to be friends, and then I dropped him, and then I feel guilty. *Boo-hoo!* Is that it? Well off we go. Let's start flying or something. Where is he? Where's Balloonhead?'

'But you know where Balloonhead is, Bunny Boy,' said Titivillus.

'Do I?' asked Rabbitman.

'You must remember asking Toady to get rid of him,' said Titivillus. 'There was no ambiguity.'

'Did I ask that?' said Rabbitman trying to maintain the laughter in his voice. 'I only meant to get rid of him from the Dolls' House.'

'You mean the Gold House,' Titivillus corrected him.

'That's what I said,' replied Rabbitman. 'Get rid of him from the Gold House. That's all.'

'Balloon-head,' said Titivillus slowly, as if talking to an idiot. 'So what happened to him? After he was got rid of ?'

'I don't know,' answered Rabbitman. 'He disappeared. He was a loser.'

'A loser?' said Titivillus. 'But didn't you want him as an ambassador or something?'

'Exactly,' said Rabbitman triumphantly. 'A loser from a country of losers. His country doesn't even exist any more –'

'No, but Balloonhead does,' interrupted Titivillus. 'He's not doing so well these days. As Titivillus spoke a terrible groan came from the settle near the fire. Rabbitman could not see who was lying on it, but they were clearly in terrible pain. 'Go and look,' said Titivillus.

'I can't,' said Rabbitman, with real terror in his voice. 'I won't,' he said, more in a gasping whisper than his usual adenoidal tone.

'Look,' said Titivillus, his voice stern and menacing. Compelled by the instruction, Rabbitman moved forward. He moved around the settle, trying to keep as much distance from it as he could, manoeuvring himself to a place where he could see the horrific sight of a man sprawled in front of him, naked, his legs wide apart, his hands tied together high above his head.

'His face,' said Rabbitman. 'It's Balloonhead. But his face. What's happening to him?' Rabbitman saw Balloonhead's face constantly morph into the faces of other people, one after the other, thousands of them, all still Balloonhead, but also all someone else.

Titivillus was now seated at the presidential desk again. From a nearby fruit bowl he had taken an apple and was eating it with gusto. 'You see, since Britannia broke up,' said Titivillus between bites, 'Englandshire hasn't done so well. It might have something to do with the stupid name

Balloonhead came up with for the country. I mean, Englandshire! Fuxit threw up some nutty politicians in those years. Anyway, there's a lot of poverty there now. People are desperate. It has become the sex capital of Europe. But you know that, don't you, Bunny Boy? Aren't you developing some properties there? Brothels and casinos I'm told. In a new batch of private enclaves. Anyway, Balloonhead's punishment, for betraying his country, is forever linked to the fate of his country.'

'What do you mean?' asked Rabbitman still transfixed by the sight of Balloonhead's face, and realising for the first time that each of the faces that flitted over his old friend's features was grimaced with terror and pain.

'We were rather proud of this one,' said Titivillus. 'We came up with an idea that every time someone travels to Englandshire to pick up a prostitute, Balloonhead is made to inhabit the prostitute's body while he or she is being fucked. You know he gets fucked hundreds of times a night now. And in every way possible. Who would have thought the Germans could be so imaginative! He's beaten sometimes too. Whatever the punters want. And every time it happens we make sure it feels like the first time for him. All those faces you see. On his face. They are their faces.'

Rabbitman was disturbed. Rousing himself again he said, 'So what's that to do with me?'

'You must remember, Bunny Boy,' said Titivillus. 'When Balloonhead asked for your help. When he asked for funds to rebuild Englandshire. To turn it into the fifty-first state.'

'So I showed loyalty to my country,' exclaimed Rabbitman. 'I've always known what loyalty means. What would Freedonians want latching on to that ass-hole country?'

'Maybe,' said Titivillus 'But Balloonhead wouldn't take no for an answer, would he? And he made a fatal mistake. He tried blackmail. For the first and only time in his life, he threatened to tell the truth. He said he knew where the bodies were buried. Then he became one. It's not really a good advertisement for your claim of loyalty.'

'What kind of loyalty did he show?' replied Rabbitman. 'He threatened me.'

'True,' agreed Titivillus. 'So you popped him. Fair enough I guess.'

'I did not pop him,' shouted Rabbitman. 'If Toady did that, it was his mistake. It wasn't what I meant. Stick that one on Toady's tab. Besides Balloonhead was disloyal to me. I have always been loyal to my true friends.'

'And your country?' asked Titivillus, suddenly wrong-footing Rabbitman.

'My country?' replied Rabbitman, unsure of the connection between friendship and patriotism. 'Yeah, I've been loyal to my country. Sure. But we're talking about being loyal to one's friends. Toady stood by me all through my first campaign, when no one else in the Republican Party would, and I gave him his reward. I made him the Attorney. And he's still there. So you see, loyalty leads to loyalty.'

Titivillus stood up and walked over to the fire. With Balloonhead writhing on the settle, the only place to sit was on Rabbitman's beloved fireside armchair. Titivillus sat himself down. Rabbitman glared at him, unsure what was more aggravating, Titivillus now sitting in his second favourite chair in the Rabbitman Room, or Titivillus toying with him. Of course Rabbitman knew he was being toyed with. He'd done it to others often enough to recognise when it was being done to him. 'Yes, there's Toady. A rubber toad,' continued Titivillus. 'You have been loyal to him, but do you remember some of the things he said during that first election?'

'I remember he said we have to reclaim our country,' said Rabbitman. 'And he was right. And we have.'

'I don't think he just said that,' said Titivillus. The television set in the corner of the Rabbitman Room flickered into life and on the screen appeared archive film of Rabbitman's first presidential campaign. On the screen Rabbitman could see Toady giving a speech.

'Fellow Freedonians,' said Toady. 'We have to reclaim our country, back from those who have taken it away from us. From the Jews and the feminists and the faggots. From the unborn baby killers. From the muslims who want to slit out throats while we sleep, and rape our women in their beds. From the foreigners who have stolen our jobs. From everyone who is not a pure Freedonian. For too long we have had the dogma of equality, multiculturalism and civil rights rammed down our throats until we have choked. Well no more! Fellow Freedonians, we want our country back.'

The television went blank again. Titivillus looked at Rabbitman closely in the hope of seeing some remorse. But he could see nothing more than an overgrown eight-year-old boy, who did not really think he had done anything wrong. 'It was an election campaign,' said Rabbitman calmly. 'People say extreme things. She said rude things about me too. She was very very rude, and she wouldn't apologise.'

'She?' asked Titivillus.

'That bitch,' said Rabbitman. 'She said I groped girls.'

'Didn't you?'

'Only those who wanted me to,' said Rabbitman.

'And how did you know they wanted you to?' asked Titivillus.

'You can tell,' said Rabbitman. 'You can always tell. Okay?'

'And the ones you raped?' asked Titivillus. 'Did they want you to?'

'I never raped anyone,' shouted Rabbitman. 'There was always consent. Always. I always had witnesses.'

'Witnesses?' said Titivillus. 'People watched you rape young girls?'

'I did not rape anyone,' shouted Rabbitman again. 'Ask my people. They'll tell you. They always wanted me to –'

'Rape them?' interjected Titivillus.

'Fuck you!' shouted Rabbitman. *Fuck you!* We were talking about loyalty. We were talking about Toady. Even if Toady said some things he shouldn't have, I still stood by him. He was loyal and so was I. That was the point I was making.'

'But the point I was making,' said Titivillus calmly, 'is that perhaps being loyal to a man like Toady is not a good idea. Perhaps it shows poor judgement. And perhaps poor judgement is a kind of disloyalty. Not to Toady, of course, but disloyalty to your country.'

'Says you!' shouted Rabbitman childishly.

'Tell me,' said Titivillus, 'was it out of loyalty that you agreed to Toady's plan to reform the country? I mean, what was wrong with the Union of Freedonia anyway? Why did you change the constitution and ressurect the Federacy of Freedonia. Did you ever think that was a good idea? Given the history I mean.'

'Look, Freedonia was on the wrong path. Okay? All I did was return it to the right path.'

'The path it left in 1865?'

'I don't know what that is,' replied Rabbitman. 'Look, I don't do history. Okay?'

'No, you leave it to men like Toady,' scoffed Titivillus. 'But my real question is whether it was done out of stupidity or loyalty. It wasn't just a change of name. I mean there were real changes to the constitution. The changes that meant –'

'Look!' interrupted Rabbitman, 'If you mean the blacks, well they were never in the constitution. *Okay?* Toady explained all that. Every day Toady explained it. The Claim of Independence wasn't written by any blacks. There are no niggers in the constitution.'

'What did you just say?' asked Titivillus.

'I said blacks,' said Rabbitman. 'Blacks. Anyway, all Toady did was give them what they wanted. You just have to listen to their music and they're always going on about living in ghettos. So I gave them their ghettos. Real ghettos. History isn't going to condemn me for giving people what they want.'

'So you based your race relations policy on some half-baked view of black music,' said Titivillus. 'Did you never stop to think the teenage music scene is not necessarily the best source to develop social policy? Or you could have just asked your fellow Freedonians what they wanted. And listened to what they said.'

'Fuck that,' snarled Rabbitman. He picked up his sarsaparilla from the nearby table and took a long swig. Refreshed by the sudden dose of sugar he turned to Titivillus and shouted, 'And fuck you!

I did ask. I asked the people. I stood for election. Twice I asked the people and the people elected me twice. That meant I could do what I liked. The people gave me power. When they did that my words had meaning. I'm the President for fuck's sake. I was elected and I did what was right. I always do what is right. I'm the fucking President!'

'That's right. You're the fucking President. But presidents are not elected to fuck. They're elected to govern. To govern for everybody. You are the President of all Freedonians. But you changed the Constitution to lock a fifth of your fellow Freedonians in ghettos.'

'Ah! Ah!' replied Rabbitman, almost dancing at his presumed victory. 'See you are wrong. Wrong! So, so wrong. *Fake news!* They are not locked in! They can still come out to work. I know because we've got some black cleaners working here. I've seen them. I've seen them!'

Titivillus looked at Rabbitman jumping up and down and couldn't help wondering how such a moron was ever elected president. Titivillus sighed. 'But they cannot live here,' he said. 'Not since the

Toady Amendment to the Constitution. Not since the Union States became the Federate States. What was it Toady said? "We want our country back!" Who did he think had taken it away from him?'

'If patriotism is a sin, then I admit it, I'm a sinner,' said Rabbitman.

'Let me assure you,' said Titivillus, 'it is a sin. One of the worst. All patriots go to hell. The trouble is they often take innocent people with them.'

'Well in that case it's Toady's sin.' said Rabbitman. 'He said those things about blacks. It sits on his head. He took it through parliament. It sits on his head. I'm only the President. It sits on his head.'

'That's not very loyal, Mr President,' said Titivillus sarcastically.

Titivillus stood up and moved to stand next to Rabbitman. Rabbitman glared at him with a mixture of absolute hatred and fear. Titivillus leaned in close to Rabbitman, as if he wanted to whisper a secret into Rabbitman's ear. 'And besides which,' he said. 'We know. Don't we? We know.'

'Know what?' asked Rabbitman, also in a whisper that not only aped that of Titivillus, but betrayed his fear at what new revelation was about to be aired.

'We know that when you asked the people, most of them said no,' said Titivillus. 'We know, you lost that first election, by three million votes, didn't you Bunny Boy?' Titivillus moved away from Rabbitman, sat himself back in the fireside armchair. Leaning out of the chair, Titivillus looked back at Rabbitman, and placed his thumb and forefinger on his forehead to form the letter L, while mouthing the word, 'Loser.'

'I won!' insisted Rabbitman, a new anger rising in him at the latest assault on his dignity. 'I won! I won the electoral college, and that's what counts.'

'That's what counts!' repeated Titivillus in mock agreement.

'And I won the popular vote too,' said Rabbitman, his voice rising. 'If you take out all the illegal immigrants who voted –'

'Illegally?' suggested Titivillus.

'Yes, illegally,' continued Rabbitman. 'Take them out and I won the popular vote too. Okay?'

Titivillus laughed loudly, and as he did Rabbitman couldn't help noticing the whole room seemed animated, as though the gilded cherubim on the cornices, and the painted cherubim on the ceiling, and the sphinxes on the candelabra, and even the chairs and tables in the room, and the roaring logs in the fire, everything in that space was all laughing in unison with the devil who had dared invade Rabbitman's private space. 'Absolutely!' said Titivillus. 'And if we take out the vampires, and zombies, and bogeymen, and the sciapods, and the blemmies, and the unicorns, then you were way ahead.'

'Yeah, that's right,' said Rabbitman defiantly, wondering what a blemmie was. 'So fuck you! I won. Okay? I won! Who the fuck are you to even talk to me?'

'Moi?' said Titivillus. 'I'm just one of that very small band who turned up at your inauguration. Plenty of left-overs for the doggy-bag from that party I recall. But I'm also someone who

wonders why you wanted power so much you destroyed an entire nation to get it. More than a nation, if you think about your impact outside Freedonia. You have definitely changed history, Bunny Boy. Changed it big time.'

'I made Freedonia great again,' retorted Rabbitman.

'Whatever,' said Titivillus sounding bored with Rabbitman's histrionics. 'I suppose you wanted wealth and power to make up for your childhood in Pakistan. It's a remarkable rise. From street urchin in Waziristan to Freedonian president.'

'That's bullshit,' shouted Rabbitman. 'Bull! Shit!'

'You know you cannot lie to me, Bunny Boy. I write the Book of Truth, so I know. And you know the truth, don't you Dawood?'

'The truth is bullshit,' cried Rabbitman.

'میز جھوٹ جھ زمین روتا' said Titivillus

'That's not true!' replied Rabbitman. 'I was born in Freedonia. My name is not Dawood. I have a birth certificate to prove it.'

'Yes,' agreed Titivillus. 'You have a birth certificate. I saw you buy it from a back street forger in Karachi. Funny how no one ever noticed he'd misspelled Freedonia.

'I'm Freedonian,' shouted Rabbitman, his face so red it glowed like an ember in the burning fire. 'I was born in Freedonia. I love Freedonia.'

'Even if you were born in Freedonia,' said Titivillus, 'I'm not sure you could ever claim you loved Freedonia. What is Freedonia if it's not its people and its constitution? But you attacked both. You are a traitor, Mr President. You betrayed your country because you betrayed your people. Oh maybe not all the people. There are a few who have grown very rich and powerful under you. But a president who betrays the trust of even one of the people is always a traitor, and you betrayed way more than one.'

A strange silence fell over the room. In some dark corner of Rabbitman's mind he wondered if that was it, whether judgement had been given. Titivillus stood up and walked over to a cabinet at the side of the room. He picked up a decanter filled with bourbon and poured himself a large glass. Turning to Rabbitman he said, 'I hope you don't mind. It's been a long night. Do you want one?'

'I don't drink,' said Rabbitman. 'You should know that.'

'I do,' said Titivillus, 'but, given the circumstances, I thought you might like to have a final drink before we go. You'll never have the chance again. Or a glass of pop perhaps?'

'Pop?' asked Rabbitman.

'Sorry, an old English name for soda,' said Titivillus. 'Would you like a soda? A last pleasure before you go. You do realise you are about to go, don't you? You know this isn't going to end well for you?'

'Isn't it?' asked Rabbitman, pulling a gun from a drawer in a nearby bureau, and laughing loudly.

But Titivillus laughed louder. 'You really are a very stupid man, Bunny Boy.'

'Stop calling me that!' shouted Rabbitman. 'I'm smart. Everyone knows I'm smart. I'm smart. I know I'm smart.'

'And yet, you still don't get it' said Titivillus.

'*Shuddup!*' shouted Rabbitman, sounding more like a camp backstreet hood than a dignified head of state. 'I've got the gun. I'm in charge. I'm in charge.'

As Rabbitman spoke a strange gauze-like curtain, translucent, like white Cyprus lawn, fell across the room, cutting it into perfect halves. On one side, still in the night, stood Rabbitman and Titivillus, while on the other it was daylight. There Rabbitman could see the Chief of the National Guard, standing over a body, laid out on the floor. The scene was animated, the figures moving, but as if caught on a slow-motion film.

'What's this!' shouted Rabbitman. 'More tricks?'

'These are not tricks,' replied Titivillus. 'That's a view into reality. You see, at the Gold House it's already morning. A body has just been found. The body of an old man. He died in the night. But it's a strange case.'

'You're lying,' insisted Rabbitman. 'I'm here. I'm still alive.'

'No, you are dead, Mr President,' said Titivillus coldly. 'That body is you. And there is no one who will mourn you. Not even Bunny.'

'Bunny?' repeated Rabbitman. 'She'll mourn me. I'm her daddy.'

'No,' said Titivillus. 'Soon they will find her body. She is lying dead in her room. In the night she was attacked. Someone assaulted her. Hurled her across the room. She hit her head. She's been lying there since the early hours.'

'Bunny,' mumbled Rabbitman.

'Don't worry, you'll see her again,' said Titivillus, making the promise sound more like a threat than a welcome reunion. 'Don't forget, she's a *bona fide* sinner too.'

Turning to the figures in the sunlit half of the room, Rabbitman rushed forward, but the gauze curtain, despite fluttering like Old Glory in the breeze, was solid to his touch. He began hammering on it, shouting at the top of his voice, but no one in the sunlit part of the room seemed to hear him. 'They will never hear you again,' said Titivillus. 'You belong to the darkness now. By the way, do you like olives?'

Rabbitman fell to his knees. 'Okay, okay, I get it, I get it,' he cried. 'I want to live again. I want to live again. Please God, let me live again.'

Titivillus knelt down beside Rabbitman. 'That's just it, Bunny Boy,' he whispered in Rabbitman's ear. 'You never got it. And it's too late for you to ever live again. Sorry.'

Rabbitman was crying now, but Titivillus showed no sign of pity. 'Why should anyone pity a monster?' said Titivillus as though answering an omniscient narrator.

Unsure whether the comment was aimed at him, Rabbitman replied, 'And how do you punish a monster?'

'I'm very glad you asked me that,' said Titivillus breezily. 'We have had to come up with something really special for you. With so many crimes to choose from, we consulted many of your old friends. Most of them are with us now you know. There no one crueller than one's friends, don't you find? Especially Balloonhead. Man alive! He is cruel.'

'What did he say?' asked Rabbitman in a half whisper. But Titivillus acted like he didn't hear.

'Tell me, why did you always use that prim way of talking about the women you molested?'

'What are you talking about?' asked Rabbitman.

'Pussy,' said Titivillus. 'What adult uses the word pussy to describe a vagina?'

'A what?' asked Rabbitman.

'A pussy, Mr President,' replied Titivillus. 'A vagina. What you can a pussy. But pussy is a naughty schoolboy's word. It suggests a kind of arrested development, don't you think? That would certainly explain you. That you are really backward.'

'I know when to call a cunt a cunt,' said Rabbitman quickly without thinking.

'I'm not sure that's a boast worth making,' said Titivillus. 'Anyway, Balloonhead suggested we add up all the times you've attacked women. It's rather a lot. Runs into thousands. And for every woman you attacked he wanted us to place a vagina on your body. One for each of the women you've groped and molested and raped over the years. Then he thought each of those vaginas covering your body should be raped forever more by a hoard of nasty little devils, all like you, so you would know what it feels like. Forever. He was never a very nice man was he.'

'Dear God!' cried Rabbitman.

'There you go again,' said Titivillus. 'Invoking a God who stopped listening to you a long time ago. But don't worry, we didn't go with Balloonhead's suggestion. We thought it was a typically sexist idea from him. But it did get us thinking. So instead, we are going to cover you in penises and balls. Hundreds of them, from the top of your head to the soles of your feet. Then we are going to let your wife, I mean daughter, *or do I mean wife,* do what you like her to do most. Suck-suck, Mr President. Suck-suck!'

At that moment there was a noise at the door. It opened and in walked Bunny. Except Bunny was no longer the beautiful young woman Rabbitman had spent so much money creating. 'We've done a little more work on her as you can see,' said Titivillus. Rabbitman looked in horror at Bunny's newly installed mechanical mouth, with sharp metal spikes where her teeth used to be, chomping up and down like a deranged clockwork engine. 'Suck-suck, Mr President,' said Titivillus again, slowly this time, to emphasise the sense of threat. 'Suck-suck. Although I'm not sure that mouth is capable of sucking any more. We'll soon see when she starts to graze on your endless supply of cocks and balls. Not much fun for her either, I suppose, but like you, she was no angel.'

'I have done nothing to deserve this,' said Rabbitman in a winging tone of voice. 'I just wanted to serve my country. I am the President, I should be treated with respect. I am the President.'

'Not any more, Bunny Boy. You are just another loser.' Again Titivillus put his fingers to his forehead to form the letter L. 'A loser,' he repeated, almost hissing as he spoke. 'You are so so dumb.'

As Titivillus spoke, the scene on the sunlit side of the Rabbitman Room came alive, and the voices of the Chief of the National Guard and the others could be heard. An aide entered the room and handed the Chief a note. 'There are reports of large crowds gathering in Englandshire, sir,' said the aide.

'Crowds?' repeated the Chief. 'What are they doing?'

'Apparently, they are going to church, sir' said the aide.

'Have the Brits found God?' mumbled the Chief more to himself than the aide.

'I doubt that, sir,' said the aide. 'It's a pretty godless place from what I remember. But what should we do?'

'You ask me like you are asking the president,' replied the Chief.

'The president is dead, sir,' said the aide. 'Who else should I ask?'

'Well, let the English get on with their own business for once,' said the Chief decisively. 'We've problems of our own.'

'And the president's businesses over there? Should we protect them?'

'Like I say,' said the Chief, 'let the Brits deal with them. As far as we're concerned, the Rabbitman Organisation is now closed.' Turning to a nearby guardsman the Chief said, 'Take a detachment to Capitol Hill and arrest Toady.'

'On what charge, sir?' shouted the guardsman.

The Chief looked at the soldier with a mixture of resignation and exasperation. 'Take your pick soldier,' he said. 'But if he asks, tell him it's for high treason.'

'And if he resists, sir!' shouted the guardsman.

'Shoot him in the rocks, soldier,' said the Chief calmly. 'Shoot him in the rocks. That'll soften his resistance. When you have him in custody I want you to take a detachment of men to the offices of *Scheissmart News.*'

'And what should we do there?' asked the guardsman. The Chief paused, as if uncertain at giving the order.

'Shoot everyone you see inside on sight,' said the chief sternly.

'In the rocks, sir?' asked the guardsman.

'In the head soldier,' said the chief. 'Every one of them. In the head.'

The Chief then turned to the aide who brought the news of the crowds in Englandshire. 'When he's done that I want you to issue a press release saying the Scheissmart hacks all committed suicide in grief at the death of their president.'

'Are we still going to tell lies?' asked the aide. 'Isn't this a chance for the truth to win?'

'Let's call it a last alternative fact,' said the Chief. 'There's no point cleaning out the Stygian stables if you're gonna keep the piles of shit. Then contact the Democratic Resistance. Tell them Rabbitman is dead and it's time for peace. Tell them the Federacy is abolished. The Union Constitution is being reinstated.'

As the aide and the guardsman left the room, Rabbitman looked on from the darkness and heard another guardsman ask. 'What shall we do with the president's body, sir?'.

'For a start you can stop calling him the president, soldier,' said the Chief.

'We could burn it,' suggested another guardsman.

'No,' said the Chief. 'That pen-pusher was right. It's time to stop the abuse and the lies. It's time to do things properly. Otherwise we're no better than him. We'll give him a proper burial. Low key, but proper. God can punish him.'

Despite the Chief's order, the remaining guardsmen seemed wary of touching Rabbitman's corpse. 'What are those things all over his body?' one of them asked. 'They're everywhere. They look like –'

'Yes, they do soldier,' interrupted the Chief. 'Yes they do.'

§9

'Are you getting ready for church like I asked you?' called Angela's mother up the stairs, as Angela sat amongst the toys.

'Yes,' lied Angela. 'Almost. Rabbitman has just told Titivillus that "There are no niggers in the constitution" so Titivillus has sent him to hell.'

The silence that followed was almost a physical presence, sweeping up the stairs, taking control of the bodies it found there and stopping their hearts for the time it normally took three beats to pass. Immediately Angela knew she was in trouble. The only mystery for her, was why. The toys looked frightened.

'Get yourself down here at once little madam!' shouted Angela's mother from the bottom of the stairs, sounding more like Grendel's mother than the parent of a little girl surrounded by soft toys. 'At once,' repeated Grendel's mother.

Angela's desire was to stay still, seated where she was, hoping the angry monster calling her would go away. But, as she also knew, delay invariably made things worse. Quickly she stood and ran down the stairs, unthinking why she was rushing toward an unpleasant fate. At the bottom of the stairs, Grendel's mother was angry. Very angry. Very very angry. 'You do not use that word,' she shouted. 'Never!' She grabbed Angela, and gave her a short, sharp and painful slap on the back of the legs. 'You hear me? Never!'

The taller toys strained over the balcony to try and see what was going on downstairs. 'What's happening?' asked the others, unable to see over the railing. 'Is Angela alright?'

'Yes,' came the reply. 'Except she's crying. She's gone into the front room.'

The toys returned to the floor and looked at each other, many of them feeling guilty for their part in Angela's punishment. 'Perhaps we should have said something during the play,' suggested Nou Nou.

'I don't see what the fuss is about,' said Rabbitman. 'It's just a word.'

'But words can be used against you,' said Bobbi. 'Some words more than others. Then they become weapons. Eight year olds cannot play with weapons, can they?'

'So are we all children?' asked Rabbitman. 'Do we all need our legs slapped when we use nasty words?'

'If we use them nastily, then yes,' answered Bobbi.

'But Angela wasn't using it nastily,' said Nou Nou. 'She was only quoting him.' As Nou Nou spoke she glared at Rabbitman.

'Not me,' said Rabbitman defensively. 'President Rabbitman. I was playing a part, remember? There are two Rabbitmans in this book. Me and him. I'm not him.'

'So why was she punished?' asked Nou Nou.

As the toys began arguing, Bobbi raised her paws and started saying 'Shhh,' loudly. 'Listen,' she said. 'We still have our story to finish. Shall we hear the end of that?'

* * *

As Manning and the local militia left Penny and Angela outside the church, Lucifer returned. Unnoticed by most people, now he no longer resembled the Archbishop of Canterbury, he pushed his way to the front of the crowd, to where Angela was standing by the church door. 'How did I do?' he asked.

'Very well,' said Angela. 'But how did you persuade everyone you were the Archbishop of Canterbury? You looked the same to me.'

'People see what they want to see,' said Lucifer. 'Besides which, you should know what powers I have been given to clear up this mess.'

'But won't they be a bit disappointed when they see the real Archbishop?' asked Angela. 'She is hardly charismatic, and presumably won't remember giving that speech.'

'It doesn't matter,' said Lucifer. 'She is not much longer for this world. In fact, you are standing beside the next Archbishop of Canterbury.' Lucifer nodded toward Penny who was busy surveilling the crowd whilst listening to the verger's fears for the future.

'And that business with the castor oil?' asked Angela. 'Is that how traditions are born?'

'Most of them,' said Lucifer. 'I've seen most of them starting. There's nothing natural about traditions. Traditions, identity, culture, nationality, race: it's all made up by someone, some time and somewhere. It's all bollocks really.'

Angela laughed. 'In which case why a dose of castor oil on Christmas Eve forever more? Thanks very much for that! It's not exactly carols, turkey and brussels-sprouts.'

'Sometimes you have to use the material you have at hand,' said Lucifer. 'But don't worry. It will soon evolve into sweet castor oil cakes. You'll like them. And they're good for the digestion. Think of it as a necessary purgative.'

They looked out over the huge crowd in front of them, still embracing, laughing and joking, looking now more like a gathering of people than a faceless mob. 'Watch this,' said Lucifer. He looked up at the sky, just for a moment, and then at the people. The air surrounding them seemed to quiver for a moment, almost as though wave of heat haze was passing over the scene, despite the bitter cold. When it had passed, the gathering fell silent, except one person, a man called Peter, who was shouting. 'Quiet! Quiet! Listen!' In the hush every member of the crowd strained to hear.

'What is it?' asked a woman standing by Peter, called Mary.

'It sounds like Big Ben,' said Penny.

'It is Big Ben, vicar!' exclaimed the verger with tears in his eyes. 'It is! I haven't heard that sound since Balloonhead suspended parliament. How long ago was that?'

'It's Big Ben! It's Big Ben!' everyone began to cry, causing another cheer to rise.

'So what time is it?' asked Mary, as everyone strained to hear the bells of the old clock tower call out the time to London once more. No one could have claimed the count was accurate, as the bells struggled to cover the distance from Westminster to Fitzrovia, even over the largely quiet city. But by general agreement it was said Big Ben had struck twelve. That it was midnight and a new day was about to begin.

'Well, you know what that means,' said Penny loudly. The people in front of her seemed bemused, but as if to help remind them Lucifer added an extra prompt to his little show. It began to snow. 'Today is Christmas Day,' said Penny. 'Today is Christmas Day!'

A huge cheer went up from the people, and everyone began to hug each other once again. Bottles of beer and cider, and even some wine, mysteriously appeared, and everyone toasted the first day of a new age, and the end of the nightmare that had been the time of Rabbitman, and Balloonhead, and Mr Floppy.

'What do you think?' said Lucifer to Angela, winking as he spoke.

'Did you just wink at me?' said Angela. 'I don't think *angels* are supposed to flirt.'

'Was I flirting?' said Lucifer. 'Perhaps I have been characterised so long as the Prince of Darkness I've forgotten how to behave entirely proper like. But I am glad you think I'm an angel now.'

'Angel or not,' said Angela smiling, 'I suspect you have never behaved entirely "proper like".'

'Are you mocking my accent?' asked Lucifer.

'A little,' replied Angela, winking back. 'But at least you have lived up to the true meaning of your name. Lucifer. The bearer of light. Isn't that what your name means?'

'Yes,' said Lucifer. 'A long time ago, and a long way from here, that is what I was called. The bearer of light.' As he spoke, Lucifer seemed lost for a moment in a memory, and a tear might have gleamed in his eye, who can say. Regaining his senses, Lucifer said, 'I know. One last trick and I will have to leave you, and your fellow citizens, to build a better world.'

'Why do you have to go?' asked Angela.

'Not so long ago you couldn't stand the sight of me,' said Lucifer, trying to evade the question.

'That was before I knew,' said Angela.

'Then you'll know now, I don't belong here,' said Lucifer. 'Not in the way you are here.'

'Yes,' said Angela quietly. 'I know'. This time a tear fell from her eye, and found its way down her cheek.

Lucifer smiled. 'Watch this,' he said. Looking to the heavens again, a quiver passed once more over the crowd, and when it had passed a young girl, aged perhaps eight years old, was carried forward and set to stand on one of the courtyard walls surrounding the church. As the snow fell, candles appeared and lit up the whole scene, but all eyes were on the girl, and the people surrounding her fell silent. Without any hint of nerves, or any tremor in her voice from the cold, the child began to sing. It was beautiful singing, a mournful carol few people had heard in years. It was a song many of the younger children would never have heard at all, and it was a miracle the child singing could ever have known it. It was a song that was to become the anthem of the New England being born that night, but it never sounded so pure and innocent again as it did on that night, sung outside an old church, in a run-down part of central London, from the mouth of an unschooled chorister. With tears in her eyes, Angela looked at Lucifer, but Lucifer was gone.

At that moment, Penny turned round and saw Angela standing alone in the church doorway. Seeing the sadness on Angela's face, she moved to stand next to her, and put her arms around her. 'Why are you crying?' she asked. 'Isn't this a happy time. A rebirth?'

'Perhaps, but I was just thinking about all the battles we seem to have fought,' she said. 'So many victims. Why did we lose them all?'

'The money was against us,' said Penny. 'But this time we won. Or we will win. Eventually. You'll see. Things are changing. Things are going to be alright now. You've made it alright. *You!* It was you who did this. You beat their lies with your truth.'

Angela smiled, wondering if Penny was just exchanging one lie for another. 'My truth?' she said.

Also available
from Friction Fiction

IN SEARCH
OF SIXPENCE

by Michael Paraskos

As an art critic he had often written that the
purpose of art is to soothe the pain of life. But his
theory faces a real-life test with a death, that of his
father, the celebrated artist Stass. Overwhelmed by
feelings of anger, guilt and loss, our hero finds
himself descending into a kind of madness in
which the boundaries between fact and fiction
break down. In a terrifying alternative reality,
where even time seems unstable, he encounters the
horrific figure of Pound, a murderous Nazi-
sympathiser, determined to get his hands on Stass's
diary and the beautiful femme fatale Miss Waites.
But as art and life collide in this moving, sometimes
angry, but also funny novel, the question remains
whether art can ever really act as a cure for pain.

ISBN: 978-09929247-8-2